T0149546

COSMIC MISFITS

COSMIC MISFITS

RAY ROGERS

iUniverse, Inc.
Bloomington

Cosmic Misfits

iUniverse books may be ordered through booksellers or by contacting:

iUniverse
1663 Liberty Drive
Bloomington, IN 47403
www.iuniverse.com
1-800-Authors (1-800-288-4677)

ISBN: 978-1-4759-5317-6 (sc)
ISBN: 978-1-4759-5319-0 (hc)
ISBN: 978-1-4759-5318-3 (ebk)

Printed in the United States of America

iUniverse rev. date: 10/03/2012

I would like to thank my family and friends for all of your encouragement and support. It means so much to me. This book is dedicated to all of you.

I would also like to extend a special thanks to the knowledgeable and supportive staff at iUniverse, my partners in the publication of this book.

Please visit me at these sites:

Facebook.com/SciFiwriter09
Facebook.com/CosmicMisfits
Twitter.com/SciFiwriter09

CHAPTER ONE

Ryan Bettencourt climbed into his black luxury car, and set his briefcase on the floor in front of the passenger seat. He closed his door and settled in behind the wheel, getting comfortable in the plush, tan leather seat. Business had been hectic that day, leaving him utterly exhausted. It felt good to be done with work. He was anxious to get home.

Ryan started the car, and backed out of his parking space. His was the only remaining vehicle in the lot; his hired help had already left for the day. Ryan placed the automobile in drive, and headed toward home.

It was twilight. The sun was setting, and daylight was waning. In another few minutes, stars would be visible in the blue sky above, and soon thereafter, blue would change to black.

Ryan switched on his headlights to combat the impending darkness, then fiddled with the radio. His eyes returned to the road as he was about to run a red light at a busy intersection. His eyes went wide, and his pulse quickened. He cursed as he hit the brakes. Had he not stopped in time, there would have been a major collision, and it would have been his fault. He sighed in relief, his hands trembling on the wheel.

Pay attention to the road, idiot! He scolded himself as he watched a blue sedan cross his path through the intersection. A woman in the passenger seat glared angrily at Ryan as the vehicle passed. There were more stares and shakes of the head as other vehicles followed. Ryan averted his eyes, feeling properly embarrassed. He waited for the light to change, then continued on his way.

Ryan Bettencourt was a middle aged real estate broker who ran a successful firm in the city. He was five feet, eight inches tall, and had an average build. Ryan had brown eyes, and his brown hair was starting to gray at the temples. He wore eyeglasses to correct his astigmatism. Ryan was happily married, had two terrific kids, and money wasn't a problem. All in all, Ryan was a lucky man. He was an ordinary guy, living an ordinary life.

Something extraordinary was about to change all that, however.

He was about a mile from his home in the suburbs when something materialized in the near distance. It had appeared out of nowhere, and was directly in his path. It started out as a shadowy shape, and then took solid form. It was shaped like a bell, and looked metallic. Its silver skin gleamed beneath the glow of the streetlight.

What the hell? Ryan thought as he quickly brought his car to a halt on the side of the road. The giant silver bell was right in the middle of the lane, and he was forced to veer around it to avoid a collision. His black Mercedes ended up at the edge of the asphalt, where the road and earth converged. For the second time in under thirty minutes, Ryan had barely avoided an accident. Ryan silenced the engine and got out.

What the hell is that? Ryan wondered as he studied the giant silver bell, slowly walking around it. It stood about eight feet high. It was eight feet in circumference at the base, six feet at the top. Ryan stared at it in utter astonishment as he reached out to touch it. It was made of an alloy Ryan wasn't familiar with.

"What the hell *is* this?" Ryan muttered aloud, his voice filled with awe. He looked around, noticing for the first time that he was the only one around. "And why isn't there any traffic?" This was normally a busy road, and there wasn't another soul in sight. It added to the eeriness of the situation.

Ryan's attention was drawn from the deserted street to a sound coming from the giant silver bell. A door was opening, sliding from right to left along its track, disappearing into the hull of the strange contraption. Light spilled out from within, illuminating the night and exposing the giant silver bell's interior. From his vantage point, Ryan could see a light blue wall and what appeared to be a chrome handrail about waist high. Frowning, he stepped closer.

Reaching the threshold, he poked his head inside. The wall was blue, the flooring was black, and the ceiling was white. The chrome handrail ran the entire circumference of the interior, cut off on either side of the door. There was a small square panel just inside the door, on his right. It contained a keypad with strange symbols on it. *A foreign language?* Ryan wondered. He frowned as he took it all in.

Go inside, a strange feminine voice said in his mind. Ryan gasped and staggered back, his hands trembling and his heart racing. *Go inside,* it repeated. The voice was soft, soothing, oddly comforting. Ryan didn't realize he had entered the strange capsule until it was too late. There came the quiet hum of the door mechanism engaging, and he whirled around in time to see the door closing.

With a groan, Ryan moved forward in a futile attempt to get out before the door sealed him in. He pounded on the door with both fists to no avail. He uttered a whimpering sound. "Let me out!" He cried. "You've had your fun, now please let me out!"

It was of no use. There was no one around to hear him. There was no car, no pedestrian, no curious bystander waiting in the wings. He was alone, trapped in the giant silver bell with no hope of getting out.

Something began to happen. There was a low, barely audible hum, and the sensation of movement. Ryan stared at the small square control panel beside the door; it was glowing, the keypad illuminated, the strange symbols he didn't recognize seemingly mocking him. He forced himself to release his grip on the handrail in order to approach the control panel. His trembling fingers tapped and poked the keypad with no result. All he got for his efforts was a series of electronic beeps.

"What the hell is going on, here?" Ryan moaned, becoming more agitated by the moment. "Whoever you are, this is not funny. I demand to be let out of here . . . now!" He was trying to sound tough, but it didn't quite come across. He sounded more frightened than anything. *The damned thing appeared out of nowhere.*

The sensation of movement ceased, and the low humming noise ended. Ryan braced himself, preparing for the worst.

"Now what?" He asked the silence.

CHAPTER TWO

The door to the strange capsule opened, and then another door opened beyond that. Ryan was reluctant to move at first, but since he didn't know what else to do, he decided to venture forth and investigate. Gathering his resolve, he took a deep breath, exhaled, and stepped across the threshold.

He found himself standing in a large oval room. The room was light blue, with a shiny black floor and a white ceiling. Looking down from the very center of the ceiling was a large, smoke-grey dome, like those concealing surveillance cameras in retail stores. Looking up, he wondered if it too had a surveillance camera behind it. He stared at it for a moment, then began investigating the rest of the room.

At the opposite end of the room where he'd entered was the main control center. There were two stations with matching chairs situated before them, and the chairs were divided by a console with more controls on it. The chairs themselves were black with silver trim, with high backs and head supports. The console and control panels were done in shades of grey and black. The control panels themselves were illuminated with twinkling lights, scopes, and monitors. Above the control panels were more lit panels, situated so that they could be reached from the chairs. Ryan wondered what purpose the control center served. For all he knew it could have been anything. Deciding to get a closer look, he walked to the control center, studying everything with curious interest. He studied everything with a curious eye, awestruck by the sophistication and intricate detail.

After satisfying his curiosity with the control center, Ryan continued to look around. On the wall to the left of the control center was a large rectangular view screen. It was framed in black, and there was a set of controls at the base of it. *Hi-definition Flat screen TV?* If it was, this was an odd place for it. *Closed circuit monitor, perhaps?* All he had so far were questions without answers.

Ryan turned around and noticed another control station, directly opposite the large viewing screen. This station was less sophisticated than the main control center, but no less impressive. There was another black chair identical to the two at the main control center situated before it, and another rectangular viewing screen built to the wall at eye level. Ryan noticed that everything in the room was built in, integrated. Even the chairs were secured to the floor. He frowned, wondering at the unique design of the room, and the sophistication of the equipment. He had never seen anything like this before in his life.

This is like something you'd expect from NASA, Ryan thought. *I'm not at a NASA facility . . . or am I?* Ryan wanted answers.

Continuing his unguided tour, Ryan made his way to the rear of the room, directly opposite the control center. The rear wall had three sets of doors; a single door to his left, behind which was the giant silver bell he'd arrived in; another door to his right; and a set of double doors in the middle. There were no handles on any of the doors, so Ryan had no choice but to assume they were automatic doors. When he approached the twin doors, however, nothing happened. Frowning, he stepped back, looking for an electronic eye of some kind. There was some sort of gizmo above the door, but it could have been anything. It certainly wasn't opening the doors.

Ryan peered in the window of one of the twin doors, seeing nothing but total blackness. There wasn't even a trace of light beyond these doors. Deciding this was a dead end, he went to third and final door.

He noticed light spilling out from within the room through the eye level window in the door. The window looked into a narrow, rectangular room, the deepest point directly opposite the door. The room had the same light blue walls as the control room, and the floor was the same; a shiny, highly polished black. The ceiling was done in a flat white. Ryan noticed glass panels on opposite walls to his left and right. Behind the glass panels stood human figures. Their eyes were closed as if asleep, and their arms hung limply at their sides. They stood on pedestals in individual compartments, which were set back in the wall. The figures were illuminated by a soft light glowing from above their heads. Curious, Ryan wanted a closer look.

I wish I could get in that room, Ryan thought. As if reading his thoughts, the door slid open, disappearing into the wall with a whisper of sound. Ryan hesitated before finally deciding to enter the room. *Go, enter the room,* said a voice in his head that wasn't his own. Gathering his resolve once more, he entered the room.

There were three figures on one wall, and two more on the opposite them. They appeared human except for one; a little man with light green skin, dark green wings, and a tail similar to a monkey's. He had pointed ears and elfin features. He was no more than eighteen inches tall, The strange creature was dressed in a one piece gold colored outfit. Ryan imagined the back must be open to allow for his wings. The little winged man was barefoot.

Ryan frowned, wondering what it was. *Surely that can't be alive,* he thought, and yet it was too lifelike to be anything but. Ryan walked over to the strange little creature's compartment, studying the diminutive figure closely. He stared for several moments, then moved on to the figure standing in the next compartment.

This one contained a tall, rugged looking black man with shoulder length black hair. The man had a thin mustache and a short, well kept beard. He was dressed in a single piece suit of some kind. The suit zipped in the front, and was light blue with dark blue trim. It looked almost like a ski suit. *Or a flight suit?* Ryan wondered. The man wore black boots. Ryan studied the man appraisingly. He was all muscle and looked like he could tackle a bear. Ryan found the man rather intimidating even in sleep. *Sleep? Is that what these people are doing . . . sleeping?* Ryan would do almost anything to get some answers.

On the opposite wall were a man and two women. The man was slim but well put together, like someone with an active lifestyle. He was all lean muscle, like a runner or swimmer. He was Caucasian, clean shaven, and had short brown hair. He wore the same style suit and black boots the tall, ruggedly built black man was wearing. Ryan studied the man for a moment, then moved on to the next compartment.

Next in line was a pretty, petite, Caucasian woman. She was about five feet tall, and couldn't have weighed more than a hundred pounds. She had an oval face with delicate features, and red hair fell to her shoulders. Small silver earrings in the shape of a half-moon dangled from her ears, and there was a single diamond stud in the left nostril of her nose. The woman was wearing a feminine version of the blue suit and black boots the men were wearing. Ryan found her rather intriguing, staring at her for several long moments before finally moving on to the last remaining figure.

In the last compartment was another woman, taller and more curvaceous than the little redhead. She too had fair skin, though hers was not quite as pale. She had a rather long face with a high forehead and a long, narrow nose. Her long, dark brown hair contrasted sharply with her fair skin. She apparently liked jewelry as there were multiple piercing's in her ears and her nose. The blue suit and black boots she was wearing seemed out of place with her Gothic appearance.

There were other compartments in the room, but they were empty. *What the hell is this place?* He wondered. *Who are these people, and why are they asleep in these little cells?* Ryan stood at the center of the room and took it all in, his gaze once again falling upon the petite redhead. He stared at the woman for a long moment, then approached her compartment until he was once more standing face to face with her.

Let me out, said a feminine voice in Ryan's head. It was the same voice that had previously urged him to enter the room. He gasped, and he staggered back a couple of steps.

Let me out, the voice said again, louder this time. Ryan groaned as he closed his eyes and covered his ears as if he could block out the sound. He opened his eyes and uncovered his ears, once more looking at the still figure behind the transparent barrier. After a moment's hesitation, he went back to stand before the woman.

Let . . . me . . . out. This time the voice was louder and firmer than before. It was no longer a request, but a demand. Ryan cried out in surprise. He wasn't accustomed to hearing voices in his head, after all. It was rather disconcerting.

"I can't let you out," Ryan said, looking at the pretty, still figure behind the glass. "I don't know how." Then, to himself, added, "Look at me; I'm talking to her as if she can actually hear me."

I can hear you, said the voice. *Now, let me out of here.*

"Stop that," Ryan said, wincing as he covered his ears again. "Get out of my head, please. It's driving me nuts."

Let me out, now! The feminine voice in his mind demanded yet again. Ryan made a frustrated sound, his expression going angry.

"I told you, I don't know how," he shot back. "And would you please get out of my head?" He didn't quite sound as tough as he would have liked.

The control panel beside the door, the feminine voice said.

Ryan looked at it, and shook his head. "What about it?" He asked. "I don't recognize these symbols," he said.

Just touch the top key, said the feminine voice.

There were two keys with alien symbols on them. Ryan touched the top key as she asked, and the keypad emitted a low electronic beep. The woman began to stir as if awakening from sleep. She stretched in the close confines of her little cell, and she yawned. Her eyes opened, and she seemed disoriented at first. Realization settling in, she looked beyond the transparent door. She caught sight of Ryan, and stared. Ryan gasped and moved back, his eyes wide and his heart racing. Her green eyes held him captive, refusing to let go. Ryan tried to avert his gaze, but could not. His expression grew frightened, while the woman's face was void of emotion.

The transparent door opened, unlatching itself and swinging outward. The petite redhead stepped out of her compartment and onto the deck. The transparent door to her cell swung shut behind her.

"There you are," Ryan said with a forced smile and a nervous sound to his voice. "I did as you asked . . . I let you out."

The woman merely stared at him. It wasn't a particularly friendly gaze. It was rather cold, in fact, with a subtle mix of curiosity and confusion.

"What is it? Is something wrong?" Ryan asked, becoming more unnerved by the moment. Still, the woman said nothing. She started walking silently toward him, forcing him back. Her green eyes were cold as she looked him up and down, taking in a his gray suit and shiny black dress shoes. She frowned at his eyeglasses.

"What? What's wrong?" Ryan stammered. "I . . . I let you out of there like you asked. Say something." There was no response. Ryan frowned. "What's the matter with you? I let you out. You'd still be sleeping in there if not for me." He continued walking backward, and she kept moving forward. Her movements were slow, calculated, determined. The woman remained silent, forcing him back until his back was against the opposite wall, and she was mere inches from him. She looked up at his face, and Ryan stared at back at her, wide eyed and filled with fear. The small woman eyed him curiously, silently, not saying anything as she continued to think.

Without warning, the door to the room closed. Ryan's gaze spun to the closed door, drawn to it by the sound of it closing. His eyes went wide, and his pulse quickened. His stomach was tight, and his breathing was rough. He wanted to run, but there was no place to go. The little redhead had him trapped. She smiled, an amused expression on her face.

"Are you going to kill me?" Ryan asked. There was sweat on his brow, and he was trembling uncontrollably.

She didn't answer. A slow smile tugged at a corner of her mouth. Actually, it was more like a sneer.

You'll find out soon enough, she said telepathically, deciding to let him sweat it out for awhile. At the intrusion of her voice in his mind, Ryan groaned miserably and shuddered. First her grin grew wicked, then she laughed softly.

Ryan wasn't laughing. He found nothing funny about this situation at all. He stood there, trembling but otherwise unable to move, wishing he could just go home. *Oh, gosh, what have I done?*

As if reading his thoughts, the petite redhead laughed again.

CHAPTER THREE

"I let you out of there," Ryan said again in order to break the uneasy silence. "Is that any way to show gratitude?" He heard his voice tremble at the end. He couldn't believe he was so afraid of such a tiny, delicate looking woman. It was her telepathy that got him. Hearing someone talking inside your head was enough to frighten anyone.

"Who are you, and why are you here?" she demanded, speaking aloud this time instead of telepathically.

"My name is Ryan Bettencourt, and I was brought here by that thing . . . that big silver bell." He was relieved to hear her speak vocally this time. He hoped she would stay out of his head from this point on.

"The shuttle?" The woman's eyebrows were raised in question. "I wonder . . ." Her words trailed off, and she seemed lost in thought.

"I was driving home from work when it appeared out of nowhere," Ryan explained. "It damn near ran me off the road."

"The Solar Flare must have dispatched it in order to retrieve you," The petite redhead murmured, more to herself than to Ryan. "Solar Flare?" She called, looking nowhere in particular, but no longer at Ryan. There was no answer to her words, and she frowned. "Solar Flare?" She repeated, waiting patiently for an answer. "Solar Flare, respond please," she stated, the first hint of impatience in her voice. There was still no response. Reaching out with her mind, she tried to establish a telepathic link. Ryan watched her curiously.

"I can't contact the Solar Flare," she murmured, looking around as if looking for something. "Maybe something's wrong with it."

"What is this Solar Flare?" Ryan asked.

The woman looked at him, but didn't answer his question. "It must be functioning on some level, though, because it did manage to dispatch the shuttle to retrieve you."

"What is this place?" Ryan asked.

"You're on board the Solar Flare," the woman answered. "Our space ship."

"Space ship?" Ryan said incredulously. "I'm on an actual space ship?"

"That's what I said," she stated irritably. Then, more amicably, she added, "My name's Autumn, by the way."

"It's a pleasure to meet you, Autumn," Ryan said.

Autumn eyed him with a curious frown. "Stay here," she said before proceeding to the other compartments. She awakened the others one by one, touching keypads and activating the units. The others awakened as Autumn had done, slowly stirring as if from a deep slumber. Their compartments opened, and they stepped out of them and onto the deck. Well, everyone except the little winged guy; he took to the air, flying back and forth from one end of the room to the other, looking as happy as can be.

Ryan watched as they rest talked among themselves, giving each other smiles and hugs. Autumn and the young man who had been in the compartment next to her kissed, holding each other tight as they did so. It was obvious to Ryan that the two were lovers. The rugged black man and the Gothic looking woman also embraced, but theirs was not romantic in nature.

Ryan wondered how long they had been sleeping, or in suspended animation, or whatever state they'd been in. Autumn had told him this was a space ship. It couldn't be anything built by human hands, he decided. He had seen thee control room and all the technology in it. Humans weren't capable of constructing such a ship. Nor was the big silver bell that Autumn had called a shuttle.

He began to entertain the thought that he was on board a craft of extraterrestrial origin. *Aliens? Could these people and that strange winged creature be from another planet?*

"Who is this?" The young man at Autumn's side asked. They and the others were now staring at him. Even the little winged creature was staring from his perch atop the tall, ruggedly built black man's shoulders.

"His name is Ryan," Autumn said. "He let me out of my hibernation chamber."

"How did he get here?" The tall, lanky man asked.

"The shuttle," she said. "Apparently, the Solar Flare couldn't revive us, and dispatched the shuttle in search of help."

"That's strange," He frowned.

"I can't establish a link with the Solar Flare," Autumn added. "I don't sense its consciousness, either. It's as if it's gone."

"That's not good." The tall, lanky man's frown deepened. Looking at their guest standing alone near the door, he said, "I'm sorry about the way you were brought aboard, sir. My name is Evan Starkweather, and this is my wife, Autumn, whom you've already met." Turning his attention to the others, he continued, "The tall rugged fella standing over there is Trevor Nolan, and the lovely lady next to him is Stella Gamma. The little winged guy on Trevor's shoulders is Tobias Winglittle." Turning his attention back to Ryan, he concluded, "Welcome aboard, sir."

"Thank you," Ryan said, stepping forward with a nervous grin on his face. "May I go home, now?"

"Home? But you just got here," Autumn said, obviously enjoying the man's unease.

"But, I shouldn't be here," Ryan stated earnestly, taking two more cautious steps forward. "It's getting late, and I'm supposed to be home. My wife and kids will be wondering where I am. They'll be worried."

"No more worried than you are right now," Autumn said, her amused expression somehow giving Ryan the creeps.

"We'll return you to the planet's surface at our earliest convenience," Evan said cordially. "Right now, I'd like to get to the control room and try to figure out what has happened."

"How long will that take?" Ryan asked.

"As long as it takes," Autumn answered.

"Relax, Ryan," Evan said. "You've come to our aid. We have no intention of harming you." Glancing at the others, he said, "Let's go."

Evan took the lead, and then Autumn, who motioned with her head for Ryan to follow. Trevor, Stella, and Tobias trailed out after them. In the adjoining control room, Ryan kept his distance as he observed everything quietly. He felt relieved they had no ill plans for him, and he could feel the fear in him slipping away. He watched as Evan and Autumn sat at the main control center and began studying their scopes and monitors. Trevor seated himself at the other, smaller station, and Stella went to stand quietly near Evan and Autumn. Tobias flew around in circles for awhile, then landed on Trevor's console, seating himself with his legs and feet dangling over the edge.

"This is strange," Evan said. "Something's not right here." He looked at Autumn seated to his right. "According to this, we've traveled hundreds of light years." At her look of surprise, he said, "Let's have a look out there."

Autumn did something at her panel, and a set of doors above their stations began to open. The doors were outer protective shutters for a large, rectangular window at eye level from where they sat. The window was huge, the width of it edging past the control center on either side, and the height of it going from the top of their stations to the overhead panels. Everyone watched as the outer protective shutters parted in the middle and disappeared in opposite directions, revealing a spectacular view of the Earth and stars.

"That's incredible," Ryan murmured in awe. "It's true. I really am on board a spaceship. And that's the Earth, and those are stars. I didn't quite believe it until now."

"Did you think we were making it all up?" Autumn asked, looking back at him over her shoulder.

"You don't understand. It's not every day we find ourselves standing on the deck of a spaceship," Ryan said. "An alien spaceship, no less."

"The man's astonishment is understandable," Trevor said, who was now gathering information about the Earth and studying the data on his monitor. "This world appears to be primitive compared to ours," he continued, "and the planet's relative isolation makes it doubtful this society receives many visitors from other worlds."

"I can assure you we do not," Ryan said. "I for one have never seen an extraterrestrial space craft before today, and most others would say the same. There are those who believe we are periodically visited by aliens, but there is no conclusive evidence of that . . . at least not publically."

"What more can you tell us about this planet?" Evan asked.

Trevor resumed his perusal of the information being gathered by the ship's computers. "The extent of pollution in the atmosphere indicates a widespread use of fossil fuels," he continued as everyone listened intently, "and they appear to be behind us technologically. The world itself is two-thirds water and one-third land mass. It rotates on its axis at approximately one-thousand miles per hour, and orbits its sun at about twenty-four thousand miles an hour. There are roughly one-hundred and twenty-four thousand pieces of space junk in orbit around the planet. I detect a small manned space station in orbit, as well as communications satellites and a telescope"

"That would be the Hubble telescope," Ryan pointed out.

"Interesting," Evan said, giving Ryan a quick glance before returning to Trevor. "What else do you have?"

"There are approximately seven billion inhabitants living on the planet," Trevor went on. He swivelled his chair around to face the others. "That's all I have for now. I've established a link with their satellites . . . we will continue to gather more information as time goes on."

"It's a start," Evan said, becoming thoughtful. "But the main question right now is: what has happened to the Solar Flare?"

"I'll run a complete system diagnostic," Trevor said, and immediately went back to work at his station.

"Good," Evan said with a satisfied nod. Then, turning to the others, said, "According to our information, we've journeyed hundreds of light years. The ship was on autopilot, but was apparently flying aimlessly, with no clear destination . . . the Solar Flare would never do that . . . something is definitely wrong."

"We'll know as soon as Trevor completes the diagnostic," Autumn said.

"Where exactly are we?" Stella asked, looking out the viewport at the Earth and surrounding stars.

"We don't know," Evan replied.

"How long have we been traveling?" Stella asked.

"We don't know that, either," Autumn answered.

"Why were you in a state of hibernation?" Ryan was curious to know. "Is that standard procedure when you travel?"

"Not really," Evan said. "We were engaged in battle. Our life support and other crucial systems, such as the artificial gravity, malfunctioned as a result. Our ship has certain self-repair capabilities, and the plan was for the ship to awaken us when certain repairs at been completed."

"Your ship can repair itself?" Ryan asked.

"It can to an extent," Evan explained. "You see, the Solar Flare is more than a space vehicle . . . it is essentially alive, part machine, part living entity. The self repairing is akin to your wounds healing themselves over time."

"That's incredible," Ryan stated in awe, unable to fathom such a thing. "And, it made said repairs but couldn't awaken you, so it dispatched the shuttle to retrieve help," Ryan reasoned.

"That's the general idea," Autumn said. Then, she turned to Evan. "Do you think it's wise to give this stranger so much information?"

"Oh, this man is harmless," Evan said in a dismissive manner.

"Now that you've had a chance to get fully awake and you have some idea as to what's going on, may I please go home, now?" Ryan asked.

"Not yet," Evan said.

"Why not?" Ryan frowned.

"We'd like to study you, first," Evan replied.

"Study me? Now listen here," Ryan stated irritably, "I've done my job. You're all awake and unharmed. Your life support and gravity are back online, and you're all safe. I want to go home."

"It doesn't matter what you want," Autumn countered. "Like it or not, you are remaining with us until we are through with you."

"Are you telling me I am to be a prisoner here?" Ryan asked crossly.

"Prisoner?" Autumn's eyebrows rose. "Of course not. You're to be our guest."

"We're simply going to give you a thorough examination and run some tests," Evan said. "Stella here is a doctor. She will be conducting the exams."

"You can't force me to undergo an examination," Ryan stated angrily.

"Actually, we can," Autumn said with an amused expression.

"You will not be harmed," Evan said. "We will do everything we can to make you feel comfortable. Please, make yourself at home."

"I don't want to make myself at home; I want to *go* home."

"You will," Autumn said. "Just as soon as we're finished studying you."

"Mr. Bettencourt," Evan began, "if we're going to have to remain here while we finish our repairs and try to figure out what to do next, then we need to know more about your world."

"Who are you people, exactly?" Ryan asked.

"We're explorers, cosmic adventurers," Stella said.

"You mentioned a battle . . ." Ryan began, but was quickly cut off.

"We've told you all we intend to for now, Ryan" Autumn said. "So, go with the good doctor and get the examination over with. Then, we'll all get acquainted a little more." She smiled, and it was the first friendly smile he'd on her face seen thus far.

Ryan looked at Stella, who was waiting for him to go with her. He looked at the others, then returned his gaze to Stella. She eyed him curiously, patiently waiting. Abruptly, Ryan turned and bolted for the door to the holding bay to the shuttle. The door swished open, and the shuttle door followed suit. Ryan entered the big silver bell in a panic.

"I've got to get out of here," he stated miserably. His fingers trembled as he tried to activate the small transport vehicle. With the exception of a series of electronic beeps and blips, though, nothing happened.

"Going somewhere?" Trevor was standing in the doorway with an amused expression on his face.

"Please," Ryan implored, "I must be returned to the surface."

"You will be returned as soon as we're through studying you," Trevor said. "Just as you were promised."

"We're not going to hurt you," Evan added, appearing in the doorway beside Trevor. "We're explorers and seekers of knowledge, not the aggressors you think we are." Evan glanced over his shoulder, and, seeing Stella right behind him, he nudged Trevor in the elbow. The two men stepped out of the way to allow Stella to enter. There was a smile on her face, and a pencil shaped instrument in her hand.

"What is that?" Ryan asked, his eyes going wide as he slowly moved backward. "Get away from me . . . I'm warning you!"

"What are you going to do?" Stella asked with an amused look on her face. Ryan's back was against the wall, and Stella closed the gap between them. "There's nowhere for you to go, Ryan. Why are you so worried? Can't you see we mean you no harm?"

"No, please . . . stay away from me!" Ryan cried, his eyes bulging, his heart racing. He felt he like he might begin hyperventilating. Stella brought the silver, pencil shaped device to his neck and pressed the tiny button at the end of it with her thumb. He felt a pinprick, and he winced as he groaned. He went limp within seconds, his weight heavy as she eased him to the floor.

"That was quick," Stella said with a laugh. Looking over her shoulder, she saw Evan and Trevor watching from the doorway. "If you gentlemen would be so kind as to bring him to the infirmary, please?"

"We'd be happy to," Evan said. Looking at Trevor, he added, "Shall we?" The two men carried Ryan to Stella's lab.

CHAPTER FOUR

Ryan awakened to find himself lying on a narrow bed. He was lying on his back, dressed only in his T shirt and boxers. Directly above him was a bright light. He felt strangely calm.

He saw Stella standing beside the bed, dressed in a long blue lab coat and matching gloves. She was administering an injection of some kind, seemingly unaware that he was awake, groggy but relatively aware of what was going on.

Ryan opened his mouth to speak but he couldn't formulate words. All that came out was a slurring of incoherent sounds. He looked from Stella to his bound wrists, then to the soft black padding of the bed. At the foot of the bed was a monitor of some kind; Ryan could see it was illuminated, but all he could see from his vantage point was the backside of it.

Stella stopped had finished administering the injection. She set the pencil shaped device she'd injected him with on the bedside table, then walked to the foot of the bed in order to study the monitor. Ryan watched silently as she studied the data on the screen. He tried to speak once again; however, his words came out slurred and unintelligible. Stella looked from the monitor screen to him.

"You're awake," she said pleasantly, a smile curving her lips.

She came around to the side of the bed, looking down at him curiously. "I must say you are one unhealthy specimen," she continued. "All that's going to change, however." She smiled cordially, adding, "I've cured all of your ills."

"What are you talking about?" Ryan's tongue felt thick and his lips were barely able to form words, but at least now he could talk.

"I'm talking about high blood pressure, too much bad cholesterol, too much extra weight . . ."

"I'm not fat," Ryan murmured, still struggling to speak but slowly getting better at it.

"No, but you are a bit overweight nonetheless. Oh, and I figured out why you have to wear these." She picked up his eyeglasses from the beside table and examined them as if they were an ancient artifact. "That darned astigmatism. Well, you won't be needing them anymore, because I fixed that, too." She made a show of breaking the eyeglass frames in half, then dropped them back on the table.

Ryan looked around the room. There were two more beds identical to the one he was in. There was a counter with a high backed swivel chair before it, and there were cabinets over head. Like the control room and shuttle, the walls were pale blue, the floor highly polished black. The equipment, cabinets, and counter were done in shades of grey and black. The medical equipment scattered about the room looked very high tech, unlike anything he had ever seen in any hospital or doctor's office before. He reminded himself that he was on an alien space ship, and that these aliens were hundreds of years ahead of humankind, both technologically and otherwise. He was greatly impressed.

"Thank you, doc," Ryan said. His ability to speak was steadily improving.

"You are welcome."

"Did you learn everything you wanted to know, doctor?"

"Yes. And please, call me Stella." She smiled.

"Okay, Stella."

"Autumn said you may have some questions," Stella prompted.

Ah yes, Autumn, Ryan thought. "I suppose she's telepathic, seeing as she was inside my head," he said. "But how is it she was able to in that hibernated state?"

"She probably had an out of body experience," Stella explained. Her body was in stasis, but her consciousness was alert. The rest of us can't do that . . . only she can. She's very powerful. You wouldn't believe what she can do with her mind."

"Actually, I would." A thought occurred to him. "How is it you're speaking my language?"

"Actually, I'm not. The Solar Flare is equipped with something called a Cosmic Translation System. It allows us to understand each other."

"But, when you speak your lips . . ." Ryan began, but she cut him off, knowing what he was about to say.

"It's an illusion," Stella said. "Autumn isn't the only one who can get inside your head. The Solar Flare communicates telepathically, too."

"Oh." Ryan shook his head, unable to fathom the concept. Another thought occurred to him, and a wash of panic came over him. "I really need to get home," he said. He tried to sit up, momentarily forgetting that he was restrained.

"We were hoping you'd dine with us first," Stella said. "Besides, it's almost morning I your time zone. You may as well enjoy some, shall we say, alien cuisine?"

"Almost morning?" Ryan asked incredulously. "What time is it?"

"Approximately four A.M. in your time zone," Stella informed him.

"Four A.M.? Oh my gosh! My wife and family must be worried sick." He groaned.

"Stop worrying," Stella told him, unfastening his restraints. "Everything's going to be all right."

"You don't understand," Ryan said. "Unlike you, I'm not an adventurer. In fact, I'm rather a homebody. My wife and kids probably didn't get a wink of sleep all night."

"You're becoming agitated. I can give you something to relax you," Stella suggested.

"No," Ryan said shortly. "I don't want to be drugged up anymore. I'll . . . I'll be all right."

"Of course." Stella smiled, adding, "Why don't you get dressed, and then I'll escort you to the galley. Don't worry, Ryan; everything's going to be just fine." She smiled.

Everything's going to be just fine, he mimicked in his mind, not believing a word of it.

CHAPTER FIVE

Evan sat at the flight controls gazing out the window at the Earth and surrounding stars. He pondered their situation, wondering at a course of action. They were far from home, lost, and their ship needed significant repairs. Light speed capability was out, and without it, it would take years just to reach the nearest star. Their home world was hundreds of light years away. Earth and the home world were similar, however, and they and this world's inhabitants looked alike. Everyone, that is, except Tobias. Ryan had said there was nothing like him on Earth.

Evan's thoughts were interrupted by the sound of bare feet on tile. Autumn was coming up behind him, putting her arms around him, and kissing him on the cheek.

"Well, this is a surprise," Evan said with a laugh as his wife continued to shower him with affection, kissing his neck and nibbling on his ear.

"Whoa! What are you doing?" He asked when she started breathing in his ear. He twisted his head away.

"Loving you, if you don't mind," Autumn replied with mild sarcasm. She stopped, and went to sit sulkily in the co-pilot's chair.

"Sorry," Evan said. "You were being sweet, and I was being rude." Their eyes met. Her green eyes held him captive.

"It's okay," she said.

"I've just been thinking about our situation," Evan said. "We're far from home, battle damaged, and lost in space. Trevor and I aren't sure how long the repairs will take, or even if we can make them. The Solar Flare's self-repairing capabilities are limited . . . the ship's probably already regenerated all that it can."

"Don't worry about it," Autumn said. "We're supposed to be adventurers, remember? This is just our latest adventure, that's all."

Evan eyed her lovingly. He felt so lucky to have such an amazingly understanding wife. She shared his love for adventure, and she wasn't afraid of much of anything. He was the luckiest man in the cosmos. His gaze went from her alluring green eyes to her pale, pretty face and long red hair. She had changed out of her flight suit into a green silk robe with a little green nightie underneath. His gaze lingered at her bare legs and feet, which were dangling well shy of the floor. She was, after all, only five feet tall.

"You look beautiful tonight," Evan said.

"Thank you." She smiled and winked. "Stella's going to be awhile with Ryan in the lab" she continued. "I was thinking you and I could have a little together time while we're waiting."

"Right now?" Evan's eyebrows rose in surprise.

"Sure, why not?" Then, raising her voice, said, "Solar Flare, red wine, please, and two glasses." An open bottle of wine and a set of drinking glasses appeared upon the console, materializing in a swirl of particles and a tinkling sound. She looked at Evan with a mischievous gleam in her eyes. "We've been copped up in those hibernation chambers for who knows how long, and there's not much else we can do right now. Let's just enjoy ourselves."

"As you wish," Evan said. "It certainly sounds good to me."

"Good." Autumn rose and filled the wine glasses. Then, she handed one to Evan before climbing onto his chair in order to sit on his lap. They sat together in the chair, gazing out the window together at the little blue world they's accidentally stumbled across.

"Beautiful, isn't it?" Autumn asked as she took a sip of her red wine.

"Yes, it is," Evan said as he held her close with one arm. "You know, it sort of reminds me of home."

"It does resemble home a bit, doesn't it?" Autumn stated in agreement.

They drained their glasses, and Evan reached for the bottle. She held her glass for a refill, and then he replenished his. Evan set the bottle back on the console, and the couple resumed gazing out the window as they emptied their second glass of wine. They talked, cuddled, and kissed. Kissing led to other, more intimate things.

There were no more worries or discussion about their current situation that night.

CHAPTER SIX

The big silver bell materialized in an open field behind Ryan's residential property. The door slid open, and out stepped Ryan with a big grin on his face. He was elated to be standing on firm ground again. His good mood quickly faded, however, as he beheld his house in the distance. He now had to explain all this to his wife, and it wasn't going to be difficult if not impossible.

"Won't you please reconsider showing yourselves to my wife, and helping me explain what happened?"

"I'm afraid not, Ryan," Autumn said from the open door. "We're going to be very busy today."

"But she'll never believe the truth," he pleaded. "What am I supposed to say that will be believable?"

"You'll figure something out." Autumn smiled smugly.

"You're enjoying this, aren't you? Well, I don't think it's very funny at all," Ryan stated angrily.

"Ryan, we want to keep a low profile until we can figure things out," Evan said, standing beside Autumn. "There are creatures out there who are looking for us, and who want to kill us. We don't know if they know where we are just yet, and then there are there are other things to consider as well."

"Such as what?" Ryan asked.

"Such as having too many people knowing of our being here," Autumn explained. "I'm afraid your world isn't ready for us, yet."

"It's partly your fault I'm in this predicament in the first place," Ryan persisted. "Helping me is the least you can do."

"Not today," Autumn said flatly. "Tomorrow, perhaps, or the next day."

"But . . ."

"We're busy." Autumn said shortly. Then, with a sneer, added, "So long, Ryan . . . good luck with the domestic stuff." With a wave and a mischievous grin, she turned and entered the shuttle.

"What about you?" Ryan asked Evan, who had turned to join his wife. "You're supposed to be the captain, aren't you? Don't you have a say in this?"

"Right now I'm inclined to go along with my wife," Evan said. "Everything she just said makes perfect sense to me. Go to your wife and do your best to make her understand. Personally, I don't know what the big problem is . . . *my* wife would never doubt my word. Of course, we don't know much about human relations, yet."

"So, that's how it's going to be?" Ryan asked.

"I'm afraid so, at least for now," Evan replied. "Maybe tomorrow, if you can't work it out for yourself. Goos luck, sir." That said, Evan ducked inside the capsule.

As the door was sliding closed, Ryan got an idea. He retrieved his cellular phone from the inner pocket of his suit jacket, and took a picture of the big silver bell. He watched as the door sealed shut, and the shuttle slowly disappeared, fading into nothingness. He stared at the spot where the transport had stood for a few seconds, then turned to face the inevitable.

He walked across the field and toward the two story house, his mood going further south with each subsequent step. It was white with green shutters. The house was situated on an acre and a half of land, the property line marked by well maintained shrubs. It was located in the part of town where the affluent made their homes. He approached the home with a mix of happiness and dread.

What in hell am I going to say to her? She'll never believe the truth. He tried coming up with a believable lie, but he couldn't think of anything. His mind was utterly empty of ideas. *There is the picture of the transport on your cell-phone,* he thought hopefully.

Ryan ascended the three concrete steps to the back door, and stood on the landing for several seconds. Then, taking a deep breath as he gathered his resolve, he turned the knob and entered the house. He closed the door behind him, and looked around at the spacious, well furnished kitchen. It was painted a pale yellow, with chestnut brown door and window frames. The grey on grey tiled floor was polished to a high shine. The ceiling was a bright, semi-gloss white. Chrome and black kitchen appliances lined the

L shaped counter in one corner, and there were chestnut brown cabinets below the counter and overhead. A big round table was in the center of the room, directly beneath a hanging light fixture.

He could hear his wife talking to someone on the phone in the living room. Her voice was a mix of worry and annoyance. "Honey, I'm home," he said. He tried to sound cheerful. It didn't quite come cross.

"I hear him in the kitchen," he heard her say. "I'll call you back later." His wife entered the kitchen, phone in hand. After terminating the connection, she set the wireless phone down firmly on the nearby counter. "Where have you been?" She demanded to know. "We've been worried sick about you."

"You'd better sit down," Ryan said with a heavy sigh. "This may take awhile." He wished the aliens would have spared a few minutes to help him explain all this. He could just strangle that little redhead right now. It had been her decision to not get involved. *And, her husband went along with it.*

Ryan seated himself at the kitchen table. His wife sat in the chair opposite him. He stared at her silently for several moments, thinking she looked beautiful this morning, especially after the strange events of last night. "I'm so glad to be home, Tiffany," he said softly.

Tiffany Bettencourt was five feet, three inches tall with a curvaceous figure. She was blond, her hair cut and styled so that it framed her face, curving to an outward pint below her ears. Today she was dressed in a cream colored blouse with a navy skirt cut to her knees, and navy shoes with a low heel on her feet. She stared back at him as if studying him, using the experience of their fifteen year marriage to read his posture and frame of mind. "Talk," she said when the silence had gone on long enough.

"I know you won't believe this," Ryan began, "so I want you to look at this." He slid his cellular phone across the table.

"A big silver bell?" She looked across the table at her husband. "What's this?"

"It's a transport vehicle," Ryan said. "A space shuttle. It took me to an alien space ship, and it just brought me back. I snapped that picture of it just now, in the field out back."

"A space shuttle," she said, her tone carrying the weight of her disbelief. "And, it took you to an alien space ship." She sent the phone sliding across the table back at Ryan, and stared at him silently for several long, disquieting seconds.

"We found your car on the side of the road about a mile from here," she said in an icy tone, her blue eyes holding a hint of anger. "What was it, Ryan, a rendezvous with another woman?"

"If I was having an affair with another woman, would I leave my car in plain sight a mile down the road?" Ryan asked irately. "And, I'm sick of your accusations regarding my fidelity every time I don't come home on time."

"It's not like it hasn't happened before," she said, her calmly stated words masking her suspicious anger.

"That was a long time ago," Ryan retorted defensively. "For crying out loud, Tiffany . . . are you ever going to let me live that down? It was ten years ago."

"It's not just women," Tiffany said. "There's your frequent nights out with the boys, your late nights at the office, and your business trips. You never have any time for me or the kids. Now, you want me to believe you were abducted by aliens?" Her ire was plain to see as she added, "You think I'm some kind of idiot?"

"No, I don't," Ryan countered. He picked up his phone and showed her the picture from where he sat, holding it up for her to see. "How do you explain this? Huh? I suppose I made this up too?"

"That could be anything," Tiffany replied sharply.

"And where has it disappeared to?" Ryan asked. "See the background? This is the field out back. The bell isn't there now . . . go see for yourself."

"No. I don't have time for this nonsense."

"Look, I'm sorry I'm not around much at times," Ryan said. "But there is no other woman, and all the hours I put in are for us . . . for you and the kids. We're doing all right in life because of my career."

"Money means nothing if you lose everything else," Tiffany said.

"I'll do better," Ryan said, feeling guilty about not being there more often. "But Tiffany, there is no woman, and I wasn't up to no good last night. I was abducted by aliens . . . whether you believe it or not."

"Right now I don't know what to believe." Tiffany stared at Ryan for a moment, then said, "I'm going shopping. There's hot coffee in the pot if you want any." She stood to leave. "You can make your own breakfast."

"Wait," Ryan said, getting to his feet and walking around the table to where she was. "I'm not wearing glasses, am I?"

Tiffany shrugged. "So? You're wearing contacts."

"No, I'm not. My vision's been corrected. Their doctor fixed not only my eyes, but my health problems as well . . . no more high blood pressure, no more . . ."

"Look, Ryan, I really don't have the time right now. For all I know, you had eye surgery." She sighed heavily, adding, "I'm bringing the kids to school. Then, I have to get to work." She started walking away.

"About the not being around part," he stammered, "I know I haven't always been the best husband."

"Or father," she added.

"Or father," Ryan said agreeably. "I will change all that."

"I've got to go," Tiffany said, brushing past him and ignoring his offer of a hug. "Give me some time to think. I'll see you later." She left without another word, or even a backward glance. The last thing Ryan heard was the door slamming.

"I had breakfast with the aliens," Ryan yelled after her. *That little redheaded snot,* he thought. *This was all her fault.*

CHAPTER SEVEN

After they left Ryan to fend for himself after he spent the night on their space ship, Evan and Autumn went to another part of town. After appearing in an alley between two buildings, the couple stepped out of the transport capsule and onto solid ground for the first time in a long time. Using his universal remote, Evan sent the big silver bell back to the ship until it was needed again. Then, taking Autumn by the hand, led her to opening at the end of the narrow alley.

Evan peered around the corner in one direction, and Autumn looked the opposite way. This early in the morning, there were few people milling about. Satisfied that no one had seen them exit the shuttle, the couple came out of hiding and took their first look at human society.

With the help of the Solar Flare's fabricator, they had dressed casually in human attire before coming down to the planet's surface. Evan was wearing a blue windbreaker over a dark blue sweatshirt, blue jeans, and black hiking shoes. Autumn wore a green sweater and blue jeans. Her running shoes were white with pink trim. Their human attire, along with their human appearance, would allow them to blend in nicely.

They were walking along the main street of the town where Ryan lived and worked. Evan scanned with his universal remote, gathering data to be studied later aboard the space ship. He was mostly curious about the architecture, chemical make up of things, and the peculiar motor vehicles the humans were roving around in. Autumn was more interested in taking in the sights, smells, and sounds around her. She took in their surroundings, happy to be able to look at buildings, trees, animals, and blue sky again. She liked the way the gentle breeze stirred the curls of her long red hair, and how the sun shone down warmly upon her face.

"This is beautiful," Autumn said, smiling as she beheld everything with great interest. "In a way, it reminds me of home." She looked at Evan, becoming annoyed that he wasn't paying attention to what she said. "Evan, I'm talking to you."

"Huh?" Evan tore his gaze from his scanner to look at his wife. "Oh . . . I'm sorry. What were you saying, love?"

"I said I like this place," Autumn stated irritably. "It reminds me of home."

"Yes," Evan said, nodding as he quickly looked around. "There are significant differences, but I can see why you'd say that."

"I swear, Evan . . . can't you leave your scanner alone for once? Let's just enjoy ourselves for awhile."

"I *am* enjoying myself," Evan said.

"Fine," Autumn said with a sigh. "You go ahead and scan. When you're done, come get me. I'll be looking around the shops."

"Okay." Evan went back to scanning, slowly walking around as he did so.

"And look where you're going," Autumn called after him as she watched him walk away.

"I always watch where I'm going," Evan stated over his shoulder. Autumn watched as he walked right into a utility pole, then laughed as he muttered something to himself.

"Try not to maim yourself," she said before leaving him to his scanning. "We'll meet up later."

"Okay, love," Evan said without looking back. At least now he was paying closer attention to where he was going.

Autumn shook her head and laughed softly. Then, she entered one of the many shops that lined Main Street. It was a clothing store. Men and boy's were on one side; women and girls were on the other. At the rear of the store was the baby section.

Autumn slowly walked through the narrow walkways as she gazed upon the merchandise hanging neatly on the racks. She wanted to get an idea as to the types of clothing humans wore for future reference. She looked at some of the dresses, skirts, and tops. There were a number of shoe styles that she liked as well.

"May I help you with something?" A woman in her thirties asked. She was wearing a blue dress with white trim. It was unbuttoned at the top, exposing just a peek of her neck. It was made of a lightweight fabric, something one wore in early spring. She was wearing a pair of dark blue dress shoes with low heels.

"Uh, no," Autumn said with a smile. "I'm just looking."

"Very well," the store clerk told her, flashing a professional smile. "I'll be at the front counter if you need any assistance."

"Thank you." Autumn watched the woman go back to the front of the store where another woman was at one of the two cash registers, tallying another customer's bill. She watched for several seconds, then left the ladies department to look at the baby items.

Autumn made a study of everything, making mental notes as she familiarized herself with how humans dressed and what they put their young in. She looked at the wide variety of pajamas, bonnets, and booties on display. Sensing eyes on her, she turned to see that same store clerk watching her. The other woman was still busy ringing out customers. The store wasn't busy this early in the day, but Autumn thought the lady could be doing something other than watching her. She sent out a telepathic probe, holding the woman captive with her mind momentarily.

She thinks I may steal something, eh? Autumn was mildly affronted. *If I did want to steal something, lady, I guarantee you'd never know.* Autumn smiled at the woman, waving innocently. The woman looked embarrassed, pretending to busy herself behind the counter.

Bored now, Autumn proceeded to the front of the store. She and the store clerk who'd been watching her made brief eye contact on Autumn's way out. The woman's face flushed. Autumn merely smiled, or rather, sneered, as she walked by the counter and left the store.

Autumn walked by more stores, peering into the windows of some, and looking at the window displays of others. She came to a restaurant, and look at the people inside who were seated at booths or at the front counter on stools. People were having breakfast, some with company and others alone. At least one patron noticed her, eyeing her with casual interest as he brought a cup of coffee to his lips. Autumn quickly scanned the place, then moved on.

Autumn continued on her way along the sidewalk, passing by shop after shop until she came across a convenience store. She had noticed shelves of food on her way by, and so she stopped to have a closer look. She peered through the large window and saw there were aisles of shelves, stocked with everything from bread to cereal to fresh produce. There were only a few patrons that she could see, and there were two clerks behind a long counter. Curious, she slipped inside.

A bell jingled as she entered. She glanced over her shoulder at the bell, then proceeded to walk through the store. Autumn casually walked up and down the aisles, studying the merchandise as she went. There were shelves containing loaves of bread, pastries, peanut butter and jams, and an entire array of foodstuffs.

Autumn took everything in, again making mental notes as she went. *Evan has his scanner, and I have my eyes,* Autumn thought. A display of fresh fruit caught her eye, and she stopped to check it out. Seeing a nice red apple, Autumn picked it up and bit into it. She stood there, eating the apple, oblivious to the customer who was standing in the next aisle over, watching her. Finally sensing she was being watched, she looked up and smiled at the man who was staring at her incredulously. He was short, round, and mostly bald, a ring of gray hair going from one ear, around the back of his head, and to his other ear. He was dressed in a gray jacket and faded jeans.

"Hi," Autumn said with a pleasant smile. "Beautiful morning, isn't it?" Then, realizing she had probably done something wrong but not knowing what, she waved at the man and continued on her way.

Continuing to consume the apple, she stopped at a cooler containing milk, juices, and soda. The milk and juice bottles she recognized, but the soda she did not. Curiosity got the better of her, and, after opening the cooler and picking a bottle of cola off the shelf, she promptly twisted open the cap and took a drink.

Autumn frowned, tasting the carbonated beverage before swallowing. She took another swig, again allowing her taste buds to do their work before swallowing. She had never tasted anything quite like it before. As a result of the carbonated liquid, she belched. It was loud in the relative silence of the store. She sensed people watching. Turning, she saw that every person in the place was staring.

"What?" Autumn asked, confused. "Is there something wrong?"

"I hope you plan to pay for that apple and the soda," One of the clerks said. He was an man of about forty, with graying brown hair and brown eyes. He was dressed in a plain blue button down shirt and blue pants.

Autumn looked first at the half eaten apple, then at the bottle of cola. Finally, she turned her gaze upon the clerk. "I have to pay for these?" She asked, surprised.

"You didn't see a big sign out front advertizing free food, did you?" The clerk responded sarcastically.

"No."

"Then, you have to pay for the food."

"But, food is a necessity."

"So is money," the clerk said flatly. "Now, I strongly suggest that you step forward and pay for those items."

"I don't have any money," Autumn said. She could feel the stares of the people on her, and she wished they would stop.

"You don't have any money," the man echoed blandly. Then, raising his voice and glaring at her, he said, "Get out of my store. Luckily for you it's only an apple and a bottle of soda. Had you pulled that stunt with anything costly, I'd call the cops and have you arrested. Now, get out!"

Autumn sighed, then walked to the front of the store. "I'm really sorry, sir," she said. "I didn't know . . ." She caught herself as a thought came to her.

"May I ask a question?" The man stared at her sternly, but said nothing. Autumn frowned, wondering why he wasn't answering her. Sending out a telepathic probe, she learned he was waiting for her to ask her question. "Is there anything in this world that doesn't cost money?" She asked.

"Miss, you're old enough to know money makes the world go 'round. And, you're certainly old enough to know better than to take something without paying for it. You've had your fun . . . now leave, before I change my mind about calling the cops."

Embarrassed, Autumn smiled weakly and left.

"Kids today," the clerk grumbled to the younger male clerk at the other end of the counter, who was busy cashing out a customer. "That is the future of America. Sad, isn't it?"

Autumn was glad to be out of that store, back in the fresh air and sunshine. She wanted to find Evan to report her findings. He wouldn't have wandered off too far considering they were apart. Staying close together was standard procedure while exploring a new world for the first time. She finally catching of him in the distance, she headed in his direction.

"Evan," she called to him as she neared. "You wouldn't believe what I just learned."

"You won't believe what *I* just learned," Evan responded. He smiled, sitting on a nearby bench. "But you go first," he added.

Autumn took a seat beside him on the plain wooden bench framed in black iron. "Everything on this planet is about commerce. People here have to pay for food." She stated the last as though the very idea was preposterous.

"For food?" Evan eyed her with a frown.

"I almost got arrested," Autumn continued, "for eating this and drinking this stuff." She held up the partially eaten apple and half empty soda bottle.

"We'll have to be very careful in the future," Evan said.

"So, what have you learned?" Autumn asked, changing the subject.

"Well, this planet is indeed a lot like home," Evan began. "The architecture is very similar, and the plant and animal life isn't so different, either. Technologically, these people are hundreds of years behind us, if not more. We'll have to be cautious about who we reveal what to, and how much."

"We'll have to select a handful of carefully chosen people, like we always do," Autumn said with a shrug. "There's Ryan, I suppose, although I have my doubts about him."

"He'll have to do," Evan said.

"He's a businessman," Autumn considered thoughtfully. "He may be able to shed some light as to why humans are so obsessed with making money." She looked at Evan. "Do you know what that storekeeper said to me when he threatened to have me arrested?" she asked. "He said money makes the world go 'round." She sounded utterly flabbergasted.

"We're explorers, seekers of knowledge," he continued. "We don't have to worry about provisions because the Solar Flare provides for our needs. We have no use for money. Evidently, this society places a monetary value on everything. If you want something then you have to pay for it." He smiled and lovingly touched her cheek.

"But, charging for food? A basic necessity? What if someone doesn't have any money? Do the humans let each other starve?"

"I should I know?" Evan shrugged. "We just got here. Obviously, they're not like us, They may look like us, but they may not share our values."

"I'll have to ask Ryan about all of this,' Autumn said, pondering the possible explanations.

"No better choice than a businessman," Evan agreed. "What I'm really curious about, though, is their technology . . . you know, their electronic gadgets, and so forth."

"So, we'll get a sampling for you," Autumn said.

"What do you have in mind?"

"Evan, how long have we been married?" Autumn asked disappointedly. "You don't know me by now? Sit here and wait while I go to that electronics store over there." She pointed, adding, "I'll go in, retrieve some items, then get out as if nothing is wrong." A mischievous grin grew cross her face. "They don't like thieves? I'll take the stuff right out from beneath their noses."

"We're going to return the stuff, right?" Evan called after her, watching her head toward the store. She glanced at him over her shoulder with an amused smirk on her face.

Autumn entered the store. An electronic sound filled the silence, warning of her entry. Immediately, a clerk took notice of her. He flashed a professional smile, and started walking toward her.

"Good morning," he stated brightly. "Is there something I can help you with today?"

"I'll let you know," Autumn replied before proceeding deeper into the store. Coming to a rack of portable disk players, she grabbed one and continued on her way. She stopped at a selection of combination radio / CD player, and took that as well. Noticing a shelf filled with digital alarm clocks, she grabbed one of those as well. She continued through the store, setting her sights on a selection of wide screen TV's and stereo systems. She saw computers and glass cases containing software, music CD's, and DVD's. Finally, she saw the mobile phones. Thinking they reminded her of Evan's universal remote, she stepped forward for a closer look. There were other mobile devices locked up in another glass showcase, but there were others in packages hanging from fixtures on a square display stand. She grabbed one of those, and, arms full, she headed for the exit.

Excuse me," someone called. "Where do you think you're going with those?"

Autumn turned around. It was the same young man who had greeted her as she came in. She first looked at him, then visually scanned the store. There were four other clerks, two guys and two young women, all of whom were busy with other customers. Turning her attention back to the young, professional looking young man, she smiled.

You never saw me take these. Now, go take a break, get yourself something to drink. The young man blinked, then came to as if he'd been daydreaming. He looked disoriented. He turned, and headed to the back of the store.

"You guys have the store," he said to the others. "I'm taking a break."

Autumn smiled. *Child's play! Boy, these humans are easy.* The merchandise in her arms, she turned and headed for the exit. She didn't get far before the alarm went off, however, drawing the attention of everyone in the store.

"Hey, stop!" One of the female clerks shouted, followed by the rush of several pairs of feet as they went in pursuit of Autumn.

"Evan, we've got trouble!" Autumn shouted as she ran toward him. Evan stood, and immediately used his universal remote to summon the transport capsule. The big silver bell appeared seconds later, stunning every human in sight to utter stillness, including the clerks and security officer from the electronics store.

"Come on! Hurry!" Evan yelled as he headed for the shuttle, door open and waiting. He made a dash for the vehicle, with Autumn not far behind. He entered, and then Autumn entered. The door slid shut, and the big silver bell disappeared. It faded into nothingness, leaving the humans staring in shocked disbelief in its wake.

"What the hell was that?" One of the store clerks asked incredulously.

"How should I know?" The security officer replied. "All I know is that they just made off with hundreds of dollars in merchandise." A thought occurred to him. "What are we going to tell the manager?"

"I don't know," the clerk said. "We should call the police."

"And tell them what? That the thieves made their getaway in a giant silver bell, and that said bell just disappeared?" The security man glared at the clerk.

"Crap on toast . . . you're right," the clerk said.

"Come on, let's go," the security officer said with a motion of the head. "We'll just say they ran off on foot. At least it's something people will believe."

They went back into the store. The witnesses on the street stood in small groups, speculating amongst themselves as to what may have happened. No one came up with anything that anyone would believe. The aliens left the humans with an unsolvable mystery.

CHAPTER EIGHT

Ryan Bettencourt sat at his desk, lost in thought. Luckily for him it was a slow day so far. Unlucky as far as business went, but lucky for his frame of mind. He couldn't seem to think about anything but his encounter with the aliens. It had consumed his every thought ever since he'd stepped out of that big silver bell after breakfast.

With a heavy sigh, he glanced at the ticking wall clock above the mantel. It was almost lunch time. He thought perhaps he'd have his secretary bring something back with her when she got back from her own lunch.

"It's twelve o'clock, Ryan." He looked up to see Heather, his secretary and office manager, standing in the open doorway.

"I know. I think I'll stay in the office today. Would you mind bringing me back a cheeseburger and some fries? Oh, and a soda? Cola is fine."

"Sure, I'd be happy to do that for you. Is there anything else, Ryan?"

"No, that'll be all, thanks." Ryan looked appreciatively at Heather. She'd been working for him these last five years. Her work and dedication were exemplary, and she never complained. He made the decision there and then that she deserved a raise. Perhaps he would discuss it with her later. *If I can ever get the aliens out of my head,* he thought. He smiled, thinking she looked great in her striped, grey on grey suit and open toed dress shoes. She was tall and slender, with shoulder length brown hair and brown eyes. She was married and had two kids. She'd come looking for a job because her husband was out of work. She stayed because she liked the job and the extra income. Ryan thought she was indispensable.

"Okay, then," Heather said. "See you when I get back." They exchanged smiles, and then she turned to leave.

"Heather?" Ryan called after her.

"Yes, Ryan?" Heather asked, returning to stand in the doorway.

"I, ah, would like to talk to you when we close up shop today," he said. "I've been thinking you're entitled to a raise. I'd like to discuss it over coffee later."

"Oh," Heather said, pleasantly surprised. "Why, thank you, Ryan. My husband and I could use the money . . . growing kids, you know how it is."

"I certainly do." Ryan smiled. *But I certainly don't know how you and your husband do it with what you two earn,* he thought.

Heather smiled broadly, then finally left. Ryan found himself watching her behind on her way out. *Married woman,* he scolded himself. *Besides, you're in enough hot water with the woman you've got.*

"Hello, Ryan." Ryan jumped in his seat, crying out in surprise. He looked at his computer monitor, and his eyes went wide. "You!" He exclaimed.

"Not a friendly greeting, Ryan." It was Autumn. She was sitting at her station in the control room. Ryan could tell by the background.

"How are you on my computer?" He asked.

"Why should I bother to explain? You won't understand it," Autumn responded in a condescending tone. "The important thing is: how did it go this morning?"

"I'd rather not talk about it," Ryan said shortly.

"Didn't go so well, huh?" She smiled smugly. "I really would have liked to help, but we've been so busy today. On another note, how's business?"

"Why do you care?" Ryan asked miserably.

"I don't. I'm just making conversation." She was having fun with him, enjoying his sour mood.

"Is there something you want?" Ryan asked irritably.

"Actually, there is. Since you're a businessman . . . why are humans so obsessed with money? And don't tell me money makes the world go 'round." She looked at him sternly.

"I don't know," Ryan groaned, scowling. "What kind of stupid question is that?"

"Because, I almost got arrested today for taking food without paying for it," Autumn said. "Oh, they couldn't have held me . . . I'd have been out in under ten minutes, right from under their noses. It would have been quite embarrassing, though . . . getting arrested, I mean."

"Did you expect to get food for free? Besides, your ship can provide for all your needs." Ryan eyed her curiously, adding, "Why would you have to take food?"

"I was hungry, and I didn't want to wait until we got back to the ship," Autumn replied with a shrug. "So, tell me why humans are obsessed with money."

"Why should I tell you anything?"

"I can help you with your wife," Autumn stated in a sing-song voice, teasing him. "Do you want my help or not?"

"Okay." Ryan shrugged. "It's simple enough. You see, a long time ago man started using currency in exchange for goods and services. We used bartering for awhile, and still do in non-professional situations, but for the most part it's money that gets people what they want."

"I think that stinks," Autumn said. "What about people who have no money? They starve?"

"No, we take care of them with things like food stamps," Ryan explained, thinking this was a stupid conversation.

"What are food stamps?" Autumn frowned, then quickly waved off the thought. "Never mind."

"You must find us very puzzling," Ryan said.

"I find you very materialistic and greedy," Autumn said.

"Not everyone has a space ship to provide for their needs," Ryan said. "It's the way things are. Don't be so quick to judge."

"We live for knowledge and adventure," Autumn said. "We explore, learn, and study things. We don't care about materialism."

"I can offer you something that will shed more light on human beings. There's more to us than materialism."

"What could you possibly teach us, Ryan?"

"In exchange for you fixing things with my wife, I'll do anything you ask. I'll . . . I'll be one of your human test subjects."

"You have no idea what you're saying, Ryan."

"Oh, I think I have a pretty good idea, Autumn. You, your husband, and your shipmates are explorers and seekers of knowledge, and I'm offering myself as a subject of study in exchange for peace in my marriage."

"Sounds like a fair deal." Autumn looked thoughtful, as if she were considering his offer. She didn't tell him they had already chosen him as one of their human contacts. With a wry smile, she finally said, "All right, you have yourself a deal."

"Good. Now, when do you fix my little problem?"

"When I get around to it."

"What?" Ryan nearly shouted.

"I'm just really busy right now, Ryan."

"You're toying with me," Ryan said crossly. "You have no intention of taking care of it."

"Toying with you? If I were, you would know it." Autumn's expression grew dark.

"I can see it in your expression. The smug smile, the gleam in your eyes . . . this is some sort of game to you, isn't it? Well, this is no game." He edged forward in his chair, glowering at Autumn's image on the computer screen. "This is my marriage we're talking about, you little redheaded . . . troublemaker!"

"Troublemaker? You have no idea." Autumn's green eyes gleamed with amusement. Her smile grew wicked.

"Are you going to help me or not?" Ryan growled.

"Yes, but not right now. She smiled smugly.

"You mean I have to wait? How long?"

"Oh, not very long. I just want to study human relationships for awhile. You know, see how you work things out?" Tobias came into view, and Ryan heard him say that lunch was ready.

"Well?" Ryan prompted impatiently after Tobias had gone.

"Soon, Ryan, soon." She smiled wickedly. "Later, Ryan."

"Wait! Come back. We're not finished." It was too late. She was gone. Ryan found himself staring at a blank computer screen.

CHAPTER NINE

Ryan sat in the living room watching television all by himself. His wife and kids were at the mall, shopping for new clothes. Dinner hadn't gone very well; they ate in silence, and Tiffany kept giving Ryan dirty looks. When she wanted to communicate something to Ryan, she had one of the kids do it. It was probably just as well that she'd left with the kids. He much preferred to be left alone right now, anyway.

As he listened to the news anchor talk about the latest global events, he looked around the spacious, well furnished living room. His marital woes made everything appear wrong. What good were material possessions if his marriage was in the crapper? He wanted to blame it on his night aboard the alien space ship, but the truth was, the marriage had been in gradual decline for some time. Tiffany was right; he had been a lousy husband at times. And, Autumn had touched a nerve when she asked about the human obsession with money. He was devoting too much time to making money, and not enough time on what really mattered: his wife and family. He was doing it for them, of course. He wanted Tiffany to have the best of everything, and the kids were now getting into their teens, meaning that college was only a few years away. Such things cost money.

"Hello, Ryan."

Ryan's gaze shifted, his brown eyes darting everywhere in search of the source. He recognized it as that of Autumn's, and he immediately looked at the television screen. She sat with her legs crossed in a plush grey chair. She was wearing a green top and blue jeans, and she was barefoot. Her long red hair was up and looked disheveled with stray curls dangling about her face. Her green eyes stared back at Ryan with barely contained amusement.

Ryan didn't recognize her surroundings. She was in an area of the space ship he hadn't seen. What he could see in the background reminded him of a den or living room. It was bathed in a soft light, and was nicely furnished. It looked cozy and comfortable.

Even an alien space ship must have areas for relaxation, Ryan thought.

"You again?" He asked crossly. "Coming back to gloat some more? I hope you're happy. Things here have deteriorated even more, thanks to you."

"That's too bad," Autumn said distractedly as she began fiddling with a small electronic device in her hands. It was red, and was emitting a multitude of electronic sounds as her thumbs worked the controls. Her green eyes were intent on the tiny screen.

"That's all you have to say?" Ryan asked gruffly.

"She's contemplating getting a divorce," Autumn explained, her attention still focused on the little device in her hands.

"Sorry," she added, glancing up at Ryan apologetically. "I'm trying to figure out why my husband is so fascinated with these games."

"My life is falling apart, and all you can do is sit there playing an electronic game?" Ryan asked, flabbergasted. "And what do you mean, she's contemplating a divorce?" His voice was tinged with dismay.

"I'm telepathic, remember? I read her mind."

"You mean, you saw her?"

Autumn looked up at him and frowned. "No. What makes you think that?"

"Don't you have to be in close contact with the subject?" Ryan asked with a confused look on his face.

"No."

"Just how powerful are you?"

"Powerful enough for my consciousness to function even though my body's in suspended animation," Autumn answered. "Haven't you wondered how I was able to communicate with you even in sleep?"

"Uh . . . not until you just mentioned it," Ryan said. "Things have been happening so fast that I haven't had time to think much about anything."

"Well, you'd better start thinking, Ryan." Autumn went back to her game as she spoke the last. "Before it's too late."

"I just don't understand why you refuse to come here and explain to my wife what happened," Ryan complained. "Is it really too much to ask?"

"I never refused, Ryan," Autumn said impatiently, more irritated with the game than with Ryan. She made an angry sound when something to do with the game went wrong. "I will fix it," she continued, "but at a time of my choosing. I told you . . . I'm studying human behavior, and you are my number one subject."

"Can't you use someone else?"

"No," Autumn replied flatly. Her attention went from the game to him. She looked annoyed. "I have chosen you," she concluded.

"Look," Ryan said angrily, "I was the one who awakened you people, remember? If not for me, you would all still be in that hibernated state, and your ship would still be wandering aimlessly through space. The way I see it, you people owe me."

"If it wasn't you, it would have been someone else," Autumn countered. "The Solar Flare picked you at random. As a thank-you, we had Stella cure all of your ills. All of them. So, the way I see it, we owe you nothing."

"So, as far as you're concerned we're even, then?"

"Yes," Autumn answered smugly. She turned her attention back to the game device in her hands.

"Well, if that's the way it's going to be then just leave me alone," Ryan grumbled. "You people can all kiss my ass. I want nothing more to do with you."

Autumn looked up with a frown. "Why would we want to do that? And why would you want us to?" She asked, not realizing it was a figure of speech.

"Just leave me alone," Ryan said.

"Be careful what you wish for, Ryan." Her eyes narrowed. "Because, if I decide to grant your request, you'll never see me again. Which means, your marital woes will have to be fixed by you and your wife, without my help." She resumed playing the game.

Ryan's demeanor changed in understanding. "I'm sorry," he said. "I didn't mean to get nasty. I'm just frustrated, that's all. Please, don't abandon me here."

"I thought that might get your attention." Autumn looked up at Ryan and smiled.

Now, you listen to me," Autumn began, her expression becoming serious. "We will fix your situation when we're ready, not before. There are people on your planet who are starving, dying of curable diseases simply because they don't have access to heath care, or living on the streets because nobody cares. Your pitiful little marriage problems pale in comparison, don't you think? Is that how all humans are? Are all humans as selfish as you?"

Ryan stared at Autumn silently.

"Don't answer, Ryan. We'll find out for ourselves." She picked up the game unit, and resumed playing. "Now, sit tight, be patient, and let things play out." She gave him one last glance. "Understood?"

"Yes," Ryan answered sullenly.

"Good." Autumn smiled brightly. Ryan didn't know if it was in response to him or that she was winning the game.

"Gotcha!" Apparently, it was the game. She looked up at Ryan and winked, then was gone, replaced by the news.

This just keeps getting weirder and weirder, Ryan thought.

CHAPTER TEN

Stella Gamma was happy to be walking on solid ground. After being in space for who knew how long, it felt good to be breathing fresh air again; to be looking at something other than stars, planets, and supernovas. Space was beautiful, but it could drive you mad if you didn't land on a planet once in a while.

Per Evan's order, she was dressed like the humans. The ship's fabricator had provided her with a black, imitation leather jacket, which she wore over a dark blue blouse. She wore a black skirt, also imitation leather, which was cut at the knees. She wore a pair of black, calf-high boots with pointed toes and a low heel. She thought the attire not only looked good, but would enable her to blend in well with the humans. Then, there was the jewelry, of course. Lots and lots of jewelry . . . she couldn't go exploring without that. She rounded out the outfit with a small black fabric purse with shoulder strap. A little research had told her that human females tended to like such things.

So, she was now fully prepared to explore. She was in the suburbs of the now familiar city in the northeast part of the United States where the Solar Flare had picked up Ryan, the area commonly known as New England. They had decided to explore and study the same region for the time being, seeing that their business with Ryan wasn't finished. They also didn't want to stray too far apart from one another, standard procedure in alien terrain, at least until Evan gave the go-ahead to do otherwise. The area did have quite a lot to offer; there was lots to see and do.

Stella smiled as she took in her surroundings, her boots clicking and clacking on the concrete as she walked. The sky above was a clear blue with the exception of a few puffy white clouds drifting by overhead. The sun was warm and comforting, and a gentle breeze tugged at her long, dark brown hair.

Like Evan and Autumn before her, she frowned at the strange motor vehicles passing by on the street. She hadn't seen such a primitive mode of transportation before. Compared to a transport pod, these things were akin to learning how to walk.

Stella turned her attention elsewhere. She watched the pedestrians make their way through town on foot, going about their business as they stepped in and out of the many shops and restaurants that lined the bustling downtown.

Turning her attention to nature, she smiled at the varied species of birds, either flying through the air or perched in many different types of trees in the area. The sights, scents, and sounds around her made her happy. It was indeed so very good to be walking on ground again. She breathed in deeply, then exhaled.

This place should suit our needs nicely, she thought.

Making her way to the town green, Stella entered the park and sat down on one of the benches. The metal frame was painted black, the seat and back were crafted of stained, weatherproofed wood. There was a large gazebo in the park; it was white with green trim. There was also a monument dedicated to the local war dead, their names etched into a large bronze plaque. Trees and shrubbery dotted the park, and there were paths for people to enjoy.

Stella sat for awhile, enjoying the fresh air, taking everything in. There were a few curious looks in her direction as people went by the park, either on foot or in cars. Stella didn't realize that her appearance worked against her desire to blend in; the Gothic look wasn't all that common in a rural area. In the city, perhaps, but not in the suburbs. People were bound to stare.

One such curious onlooker was a young man on a bicycle. He was riding by the place where Stella sat, and he was instantly captivated by her. Their eyes met briefly, and the young man of about twenty waved as he continued on, staring at her over his shoulder. Stella smiled and waved back.

Not paying attention to where he was going, the young man nearly collided with a young mother pushing a baby carriage. He swerved to avoid contact, and in so doing, lost control of his bike. He ended up lying in a heap on the side of the road, his bicycle lying beside him. He groaned at the sensation of pain, slowly getting first to his knees, and then to his feet. Stella watched him nursing his shoulder as he tried to walk it off. Not thinking, he was walking in tight circles in the road. He didn't see the oncoming car. The driver of the oncoming car didn't see him until it was too late. There was the sound of squealing tires as the driver hit the brakes hard. The young man was struck by the car, sending him airborne until he landed on the pavement several feet away. He struck the road hard, rolling over several times before coming to an abrupt halt.

Stella stood and watched, her brown eyes pinched in worry. He wasn't moving. Concerned, she ran toward where he lay. It wasn't easy running in boots, either; especially boots with three inch heels. But, she was determined to render whatever assistance she could. He quite possibly needed a doctor, and she was, after all, a doctor. He had been staring at her; she though blameless, she felt partly responsible.

By the time she got to the accident scene, the driver of the blue sedan was out and standing over the young man, who was moaning and groaning as he rolled around on the pavement. The driver's female passenger was also standing over the young man, nagging to her male companion about keeping his eyes on the road and paying closer attention. A crowd of curious bystanders was beginning to grow, and people passing by in automobiles in the opposite lane gawked on their way by. The other lane, of course, had come to a standstill, the traffic beginning to back up.

Stella lowered herself to a crouch beside the hurt young man. He was lying on his back now, gazing up at her with a pained expression. She caressed his face with one hand, her other hand on his shoulder.

"Try to relax," she told him. "It's going to be all right. I'm a doctor." He nodded weakly as she retrieved her medical scanner from her purse. She then began to scan him, the little black and silver device emitting soft electronic noises as she did so.

"What is that?" The driver of the vehicle that had struck the young man asked. "Some new medical contraption they invented?"

"You said you're a doctor?" His female companion asked, her expression one of great concern. "Please help him. My boyfriend should have been paying closer attention to the road."

"He'll be all right," Stella said, her gaze on the monitor screen as she spoke. "In addition to the lacerations, there's some internal damage and head trauma . . . I'll have to get him somewhere I can work on him, quickly."

"She doesn't look like a doctor," the man said.

"David, shush," his girlfriend whispered, jabbing him in the side with an elbow.

"Well, look at her. She looks like someone who hangs around at a Goth club."

Stella glanced up at the man, ignoring his stereotypical comment. She then dug in her bag for her universal remote. Then, after tucking her medical scanner away, she summoned the transport module with a touch of the keypad. The giant silver bell materialized shortly thereafter.

There were gasps and low murmurings from the steadily increasing crowd as they beheld the alien contraption, which was standing at the ready a few feet away in the road. There came the sound of sirens in the distance, growing louder as emergency vehicles neared the scene. Stella would have to act quickly.

"What's your name, hon?" She asked the ailing accident victim.

"Braden," the young man croaked, wincing in pain.

"Come on, Braden, let's get you out of here. I'm going to take good care of you."

The door of the giant silver bell slid open. Stella then grabbed Braden beneath the shoulders, and dragged him inside. Stella caught sight of people pointing their mobile devices at the giant silver bell, and of her dragging Braden inside it. She had no way of knowing they were recording everything. Even if she had, she had no time to worry about it; she needed to get Braden aboard the Solar Flare as quickly as possible.

The door slid shut, and the transport capsule slowly faded into nothingness. All that remained was an empty spot and a memory of the strange, alien vehicle. The murmurings of the large crowd of humans grew more and more animated as the spectacular sight unfolded before their eyes. Emergency vehicles arrived at the scene at last. By then, though, the big silver bell had already vanished.

Stella gently eased Braden onto his back, his nearly six foot frame stretching nearly wall to wall in the transport's interior. He moaned and groaned, his head slowly moving from side to side. His eyes were opening and closing, and his face was a mask of utter discomfort.

"Hang on, Braden," Stella said as she caressed his face with the back of her left hand. Her right hand was resting on his shoulder in a comforting gesture. "I'll get you well in no time . . . I promise." Braden was making incoherent noises. He was going into shock.

The transport capsule materialized in the corridor outside the entrance to the infirmary. It barely fit. There was just enough room for someone to squeeze between it and the wall on either side, and there was no more than a few inches between the top and the ceiling.

Stella spoke into the microphone in the silver bracelet on her right wrist. "Evan, Trevor . . . I need immediate assistance at the infirmary."

"On my way," came Evan's response over the speaker on the opposite side of the bracelet.

"Be right there," Trevor said soon thereafter.

As she pressed the button to manually open the door to the transport capsule, Stella stooped over Braden with a concerned expression on her face. He looked up at her, in obvious pain by his own expression. He reached out and grabbed her forearm.

"It's okay, Braden. I'm going to take care of you," she said sympathetically.

"What have we here?" Evan asked from where he stood in the doorway. Trevor stood just behind him, looking over his shoulder at Braden with curious interest.

Stella looked up Evan. "His name is Braden. He was struck by a motor vehicle, and is badly hurt," she explained.

"Why didn't you leave him to the human care givers?" Evan asked.

"They were taking too long. He needs immediate attention." Stella got to her feet. "Besides, he was hurt because he was watching me instead of paying attention to where he was going. I feel partly responsible."

Evan looked from Stella to Braden, then back at Stella. He sighed. "All right. Let's get him in the infirmary." He looked at Trevor. "Let's wheel a bed out here for him."

Trevor nodded, and went silently on his way. He returned a moment later with a medical bed on wheels. He left it at the door, then helped Evan lift Braden onto it. The two men then wheeled the patient inside the infirmary. They brought him to the nearest data port, and Stella plugged the bed in while the two men positioned the bed.

"Thanks, guys," she said as she went to the foot of the bed and switched on the monitor.

"Not a problem," Trevor said.

"You're welcome," Evan said as they started to leave, adding, "Let me know how it goes."

"I will." When Evan and Trevor reached the door, she said, "Evan?"

"Yes?" He paused at the open door, and turned to face her. Trevor looked on silently.

"Since he's here and we're looking to select a few humans to interact with . . ." Her words trailed off, her question obvious.

"I guess that would be all right," Evan said. He looked at Braden. "Take care of your patient." Then, he and Trevor left the infirmary.

Stella first administered something for pain. Then, she gave him something to make him sleep. Lying there on the bed, Braden looked bewildered, shock mixed with pain. He looked terrible. His brown hair was disheveled and matted with blood; there were several cuts and contusions on his face and hands; and, his denim jacket was torn and stained with blood on both sleeves. Stella looked down on him with pity. He looked up at her, his brown eyes pleading.

Standing at the foot of the bed, she studied his vitals while she waited for the medicines to take effect. She made mental notes, then came around to the side of the bed. His eyelids were getting droopy, closing and opening as the sedative took hold. His pain likewise started to abate as a result of the powerful pain medicine. Satisfied, Stella got to work.

She began by removing his denim jacket. It was quite a task as a result of his injuries, the blood causing the fabric to stick in spots. His shirt was worse, and his T-shirt was the worst. The cotton fabric was more red than white, and she had to cut it in spots in order to remove it.

The remainder of his clothes were much easier to remove. She took off his tattered running shoes, blue jeans, and socks. Leaving his boxers on, she administered to him. She cleaned the wounds with antiseptic, then closed the wounds using a small, silver, cylindrical wand that no human doctor would have. Closing wounds with stitches would be considered not only archaic, but downright barbaric by Stella's standards. In fact, everything she did and everything she used to treat Braden was hundreds of years ahead of humanity. His recovery time would be remarkably quicker as a result. Braden was totally out of it, oblivious as to what was going on.

Stella prepared a basin of warm, soapy water, and then cleaned him up. She took her time, gently and meticulously bathing his light skin. She studied him appraisingly, her eyes slowly taking in every inch of him. He was tall and rather slender, his physique like that a of runner or swimmer, all lean muscle. He wasn't a hairy man, having only light growth on his chest, arms, and legs. His face was clean shaven, and his dark brown hair was medium length for a man. Her eyes drifted lower, lingering on his private area. She stared at his blue boxers for some time before finally pulling her gaze back up to his face. She thought him quite handsome, actually, in a plain, guy next door sort of way.

"Rest, Braden," she murmured softly. "You're all patched up, and now all you need is rest." He was still out, resting comfortably, and didn't hear a word she said. It didn't matter. It was all part of her process. It was how she healed.

"Evan, where are you?" She spoke into her bracelet again.

"I'm in the engine room with Trevor. We're working on repairs."

"I'm done with Braden," Stella said as she returned to her office. "He's resting, asleep, and his vitals are being monitored. Do you want my report now, or would you rather wait so you can work?" She sat at her desk, which was built into the wall like most of the other furnishings on the ship. Everything was integrated as though carved out of one huge chunk of raw material. It had to be that way in case the artificial gravity happened to fail. Her office was small, as comfortable as it was functional.

"Sounds like I have most of the information I require, for now," Evan replied. "Is there anything else?"

"No, not really. I would like to conduct a full examination when he awakens, if you don't mind. I'd like to compare the results with Ryan's."

"Do whatever you wish," Evan said. "As long as he's going to be one of our human contacts, we may as well learn as much about him as we can."

"Okay. Is there anything else?" Stella asked.

"No, that'll be all for now. Trevor and I have a lot of work."

"Okay, Evan . . . later." She terminated the connection.

I think I will do whatever I want, Evan, seeing as I have your permission, Stella thought with a smile. Her thoughts drifted to Braden. She really was attracted to him. She couldn't help having some rather naughty thoughts about him.

Don't rush things, Stella, she thought. *All in good time.*

CHAPTER ELEVEN

"Well, well," Stella said with a smile as Braden awakened much later. "How are you feeling?"

"Uh . . . good. Great, actually." Braden's speech was still thick with sleep. He looked around the room at all the alien medical equipment and monitors. The room was bathed in a soft, comfortable light, and he found the decor soothing in spite of it being a medical facility.

"Good." Stella's smile brightened. "Very, very, good."

Braden realized he was wearing only his boxers, and only a blanket covered his otherwise exposed skin. He was very self-conscious about his body, and his appearance in general. He knew what he saw when he looked in a mirror. He was an average looking guy with an average body. Stella, on the other hand, was a very beautiful woman. He found her quite intimidating to say the least. There was no way he was getting dressed in front of her.

"Where am I?" He asked, studying his surroundings.

"You're aboard the Solar Flare. This is the infirmary."

"Solar Flare?" Braden frowned.

"Our space ship." When she saw his skeptical expression, she said, "Really. Get dressed and I'll show you. I'll be waiting in my office." She turned and entered the adjoining room.

Braden climbed out of bed, getting to his feet. He felt woozy and a little numb, the result of the strong medicines. When he finally steadied himself and was able to stand without leaning on something for support, he got dressed. He noticed that the clothes were new. It was the exact same outfit, but the garments were new. His gaze kept going to Stella's office, hoping she didn't come back out before he finished. After he was fully dressed, he sat in a nearby chair and put on his new athletic shoes.

"Okay . . . I'm all set," he said when he was lacing them up. When she entered the room once again, he added, "That was some really powerful stuff you gave me . . . I feel kinda funny."

"It'll wear off in awhile. I wanted to make sure you remained asleep while I worked on you, and I wanted to make sure you were free of pain."

"Thanks. Thanks for everything, including the new clothes. They're identical to the ones I had."

"Our fabricator manufactured your clothes while you were sleeping."

"Uh, I never did get your name." He stood up slowly, grabbing onto the arms of the chair for support. He experienced a minor dizzy spell as he got to his feet.

"I'm Stella . . . Stella Gamma." She smiled. "I'm from a planet called Celtica. I'm a doctor, as you've probably already figured out."

"You're an alien," Braden said. He stared at her, his brown eyes wide. "I was hit by a car . . ." He frowned, adding, "Then I remember you were there, and that thing . . . that big silver bell . . . I thought I was imagining it."

"No, it was real," Stella said with a laugh. "You're actually very lucky. It could have been much worse. You really should have been paying attention instead of staring at me."

"I know." Braden felt his cheeks flush.

"Would you like to see something spectacular?" Stella asked. "I'll take you up to the arboretum. There's a skylight where you can see the stars, and there's a large variety of plant and animal life. It's peaceful and relaxing. I go up there sometimes when I want to think or be around nature during a long flight."

"Sure, sounds great."

"Good. Follow me, then." Stella offered a hand, and Braden eventually took it. He was hesitant at first. He felt himself blushing again.

"Don't be shy, Braden. You're among friends here."

Stella led Braden into the corridor. It was ten feet wide and eight feet from floor to ceiling. The walls were smoke grey, ceiling white, and the floor, like every other floor on the space ship, was a highly polished black. The lighting was soft and soothing, emanating from within the glossy white ceiling. He couldn't see any lighting fixtures of any kind; only the light itself. He wondered what sort of beings they were to possess such technology.

"After you," she said, gesturing to a transparent tube on the left wall about halfway down the corridor. The tube housed an elevator which led to an upper deck. Braden looked at the transparent tube, then back at Stella.

"Go ahead, get in," she said. "I'll be right behind you." The door opened, sliding around until coming to a rest behind the tube.

They rode the elevator up to the top level. What he saw when he arrived at the upper deck was nothing less than breathtaking. It was the most incredible botanical garden he'd ever seen. The countless species of plants were alien, of course. There was nothing on Earth like them. There were vines, flowers of various shapes and colors, large shrubs, cacti, and some that Braden had nothing to compare to. All he could say was that they were exotic, and had originated on some distant planet.

Braden stepped onto the deck, and waited for Stella to join him. There were many scents and sounds. He could hear water trickling somewhere, and he finally saw a gigantic fountain at the center of it all. There were bird feeders and bird baths, and Braden eyed the alien birds with wide-eyed interest.

"Do you like it?" Stella asked.

"This is amazing," Braden replied. He looked up to see a huge, circular cupola, revealing a spectacular view of the stars. The room itself was circular, as large as two football fields situated side by side. Artificial light illuminated the gigantic arboretum.

"The Solar Flare's central clock provides a day and night atmosphere," Stella said as they walked. "The intensity of light changes to give the animals and plants a sense of night and day. This is where I come when I want to be alone in order to think, or to just be around nature. It helps keep you sane during those long space voyages."

"You have one amazing space ship." Braden said, still trying to take it all in. "Fabricator, botanical garden, a state of the art infirmary . . . and all the comforts of home."

"Not to mention the Cosmic Translation System, which enables us to understand each other," Stella said. "The Solar Flare is amazing. It's the most sophisticated, technologically advanced space craft in existence. It's part machine, part living entity."

"Really?" Braden couldn't fathom such a thing. "From what I've seen so far, I'd say you people are centuries ahead of us."

Stella had nothing to say to that. According to what they had learned about Earth so far, however, she would have to say he was one-hundred percent correct.

"I'm glad you're impressed," she said after they seated themselves on a bench just big enough for two.

He made a small noise of acknowledgment as he examined a large bush with brilliant flowers with blue, red, and yellow petals. Each petal was a different color, as if the bush itself was some sort of hybrid. Or, Braden thought, this is merely the type of thing that grows on this planet Celtica? He didn't know much about such things . . . he wasn't a gardener. His mother was, but he wasn't. He didn't know the first thing about plants.

They continued walking through the garden, seeing the sights, listening to the sounds, and taking in the various aromas. They came upon a white concrete bench nestled among the plants, and sat down. Braden was a little nervous, and clasped his hands as they rested in his lap to stop them from trembling. Stella was so beautiful. When their eyes met, there were butterflies in his stomach. He wished he wasn't so intimidated by her. He really liked her, and wanted to get to know her better, but he couldn't stop wondering why she was interested in him. She had done her job; she had taken care of his injuries like any good doctor would. So, why didn't she just return him to Earth? Why was she going through all of this? No human girl of her caliber had *ever* given him a second glance.

"What is that?" Braden asked as he saw something staring at him from within a thick bush. All he could see was a pair of glowing red eyes. The pupils were black.

"We call him Red Eye," Stella said.

"What is it? An animal of some kind, I suppose?" He could almost reach out and touch it, but he dared not get any closer for some reason. It was something about the way the eyes were staring at him. They gave him the willies.

"You don't really want to know what he is . . . I get the feeling he's making you nervous."

Braden felt a tug at his leg. He looked down and cried out as he saw a bright green vine with multi-colored flowers and thorns climbing up his leg, wrapping itself around him. Another similar vine came down from above, and started wrapping around his upper torso. He froze, becoming tense and very frightened. Within seconds, his left leg and upper body were completely and tightly wrapped in the vines.

"Stella!" He cried in a panic.

"Relax, Braden. The more you fight them, the tighter they'll become. They think you want to play." She touched his wrist and smiled reassuringly.

Then, speaking to the vines, she said, "Leave him alone, Flora. You're frightening our guest."

Braden looked at Stella in utter shock and disbelief. She was talking to the vines. She was calm, amused, and literally talking to the vines. What really got Braden most of all, however, was that the vines were actually obeying her. They were retreating, unwinding themselves from him, returning to their former state of rest.

"W-what kind of place is this?" Braden asked, his voice breathy. "Big glowing eyes staring out from within a bush . . . vines that attack people? Y-you said it was peaceful and serene. I know you're an alien and all, but . . ."

"The vines meant you no harm, Braden. Neither does Red Eye. You're simply a curiosity to them, that's all. We don't get many visitors."

Braden looked at Stella as if she may be crazy. She looked right at home here among the strange glowing eyes and crawling vines that obeyed her orders. She stood there in her long black dress and black boots, with enough sparkle in her ears, wrists, and nose to fill a small showcase in a jewelry store. Her pale skin and dark brown hair contrasted sharply, adding to her Gothic appearance.

Stella eyed him warily, wondering whether or not he was spooked enough to run away, or demand to be taken back to earth. She didn't want him to be frightened; she didn't want him to run away, or want to be returned home. She had to act fast if she intended to keep him around.

"Are you all right, Braden?" She asked. "I didn't mean to scare you. I want you to feel at home here."

"I'm not scared," he lied, keeping his voice low so it wouldn't tremble. "I'm just . . . overwhelmed, I guess. I mean, it's not every day we humans meet aliens from another planet." At least, he hoped so. He really liked her, and wanted to get to know her better. He decided to trust her. She did, after all, administer medical care to him. She provided new clothes. She was going out of her way to be nice and friendly. She apparently liked him. He could see it her gaze. *But why?* Braden wondered. She must have been in space too long . . . she must be a lonely girl, that's all, he told himself. That must be it.

Stella smiled, wanting to put him at ease. She offered her hand. He hesitated, then finally took it. A strange feeling of calm came over him.

"H-how are you doing that?" He asked.

"Doing what?" She knew exactly what he meant.

"Whenever you touch me, I feel calm. I feel . . . good."

"There's a certain power in my touch," she said. "I was born with it. I heal with it sometimes, especially when the patient is near death."

"I wasn't near death, was I?"

"No. I was able to take care of you with medicines and laser technology."

"Your shipmates . . . are they as gifted as you?"

"Yes. We are all gifted, as you call it. Each of us as a different gift, though. You'll meet them all later. Right now, I'd like to treat you to dinner. Are you hungry, Braden?"

"As a matter of fact, I'm starved."

"Good. Come on, then . . . let's go to the galley where you can sample some Celtican cuisine." She offered her hand once again, and Braden took it. As they exited the botanical garden, he kept looking back as if expecting some creature with glowing amber eyes chasing after him. Either that, or the vines.

He couldn't get to the exit fast enough.

CHAPTER TWELVE

Tobias Winglittle was awakened by the sound of someone calling his name. He recognized the voice as belonging to Trevor. He did not sound happy.

"Wake up, you lazy louse!" Trevor was saying, shaking the little winged man to rouse him from sleep.

"Hey, what's the idea, waking me from my nap?" Tobias complained. He was lying on a set of pillows on the floor of the engine room.

"You're supposed to be doing maintenance work," Trevor barked. "You can waste your time taking naps later."

"Naps are not a waste of time; they are both beneficial and necessary, especially the way you wake me work around here."

"If you don't like it you can take it up with Evan. He's the one who wanted you to help me with the maintenance duties."

"Maybe I will," Tobias retorted crossly. "I've been meaning to talk to him about expecting too much from me."

"Expecting too much?" Trevor's eyebrows rose in disbelief. "If anything, he's too easy on you. If I were in charge, you'd be doing double the workload you have now."

"Well, you're not in charge, so I'll see you later." Tobias took to the air and headed for the exit.

"Fine. Begone with you, you lazy overgrown fly. I'll finish the work without your help," Trevor yelled after him. Tobias looked over his shoulder as he left, but made no reply. The door closed behind him with a whisper of sound.

Tobias went to the control room looking for Evan. He wasn't there. Neither was Autumn. The two were nearly inseparable; you seldom saw one without the other. He wondered where they were.

"Maybe they went down to the planet in order to enjoy themselves again," Tobias muttered to the stillness. The only response was the incessant electronic sounds and blinking lights of the control systems around him.

"Maybe I'll go down to the surface myself," he grumbled. "Why should they be the only ones having a good time?" He went to the transport module's holding bay. He entered when the door slid open, and entered the big silver bell after that. The doors closed, and he activated the transport. A moment later, he was on the surface of the planet.

He materialized in the open field behind the homes where Ryan Bettencourt and his neighbors lived. The shuttle had been programmed to automatically land at this location for the time being. The field was surrounded by woods and residential properties, and was fairly secluded. The space travelers from Celtica could come and go as they pleased with little risk of being seen. It was either the field, or in narrow alleys between buildings in the downtown district. Those were Evan's orders.

Tobias flew out of the big silver bell, then used his universal remote to send it back to the ship. Then, he took cover in a nearby pine tree. He perched himself on a lower branch and surveyed the area.

The others were right; this planet was similar to Celtica, with some naturally occurring differences. The sky was blue, the grass was green, and the trees, though quite different from those back home, added a significant beauty to the landscape.

Tobias heard birdsong. He looked around, and saw a flock of little winged creatures passing by overhead. They were flying in formation. They were of a different species than the birds of home, but reminded him of home just the same. He smiled, and took to the air himself.

Tobias had been told by Evan and Autumn that there were no little winged people on this planet. That was one of the reasons they didn't want him venturing down by himself. He would be careful.

Tobias was drawn to the sound of music. His extraordinary hearing ability enabled him to hear it even from a great distance. He homed in on the sound, and landed in another pine tree near the woods, several acres west of where he started. There, perched on a branch in another tree not far from where he was, was a young boy of about fifteen. He had a small radio with him, and he was listening to music.

"Hello there!" Tobias called out. The teenage boy looked around, startled. Though his eyes scanned a the area intently, he didn't see Tobias in the tree just across the way.

"Over here, directly in front of you," Tobias yelled. The lad looked around some more, finally setting sight on the little winged man. Tobias was indeed difficult to pick out amongst all the greenery, with his olive green skin, dark green wings, and his camouflage outfit.

The boy's eyes widened, and he couldn't stop staring at the strange winged creature. He noticed the peculiar looking visitor also had a tail; long and curled up at the end, like that of a squirrel monkey.

"Who are you?" The teen lowered the volume on his radio. "Or should I say, *what* are you?"

"I'm Tobias. What's your name?"

"Jeremy."

"Nice to meet you, Jeremy." Tobias flew out of the pine tree and hovered as if by magic not far from Jeremy's tree. He was at eye level with the boy.

"Where did you come from?" Jeremy asked, dropping down from the tree in order to study Tobias closer.

"From a planet five hundred light years from here," Tobias said. He held Jeremy's gaze. Jeremy stared back at the little winged man's amber eyes.

"We're lost," Tobias continued. "We don't know where we are, or how long we've been traveling. Our ship is in need of repair, and we're not even sure if we can go back home."

Jeremy couldn't believe his ears or his eyes. He blinked long and hard, half-wishing Tobias wouldn't be there when he opened his eyes. He was. Jeremy was understandably unsettled. He told himself he was imagining it, or that he was actually asleep, and Tobias was merely a dream. It was no dream; Jeremy was wide awake, and Tobias positively real.

"No one would ever believe this," Jeremy said. "They'd laugh at me, call me a freak. My parents would have me locked up."

"Then, I guess I can trust you not to tell anyone." Tobias smiled, then giggled in a way that reminded Jeremy of what a leprechaun might sound like. Tobias wasn't a leprechaun, however . . . he wasn't even remotely like one.

Jeremy checked the time on his mobile phone. His eyes went wide, and he looked alarmed. "Oh, no! I've lost track of time . . . my chores." He looked at Tobias, adding, "I've got to go. It was great meeting you."

"Wait!" Tobias yelled before chasing after him. "We've only just gotten acquainted . . . forget your chores."

"I can't. If I don't get them done, my father will be angry. He's very mean when he's angry." Jeremy was walking hurriedly, then jogging at times, then back to walking hurriedly. Tobias had little trouble keeping up.

"Hey, I know what you're going through," Tobias said, flying at Jeremy's side. "I'm overworked and underappreciated, myself. That's why I came down to the surface. You wouldn't believe how much they expect me to do."

"You should leave. No human has ever seen anyone like you. You'll cause a mass panic or something."

"Nonsense. Who would be afraid of a little person like me?"

"You don't understand. We're not used to having alien visitors. You'll cause a stir, people will overreact, and you'll find yourself on the internet and the t.v. and stuff."

"You sound just like them. Stop worrying, Jeremy. It'll be all right . . . let's talk for awhile. You can teach me about human beings."

"Teach you?" Jeremy slowed at last, looking at Tobias with a frown.

"Sure. I said I was an explorer, didn't I? What do you think explorers do? We study people, places, and things."

"I can't. I have work to do. If I don't do it, I'll be punished."

"Punished?" The word took Tobias by surprised. "You'll by punished?"

Jeremy stopped. They had reached the rear of his family's property. It was a nice home, expensive, right next door to the Bettencourt family.

"That's right," he told Tobias. "Now, please go. I . . . I wish I could spend more time with you." Then, appearing a little sad, Jeremy turned and walked away.

"Wait! Jeremy . . ." Tobias flew to a nearby tree at the rear of the property so he could observe covertly. One of his duties on their many voyages was surveillance. His diminutive size and ability to camouflage himself made him the perfect little spy. His services had come in handy on many occasions. He'd saved all their butts more than once doing surveillance work and other covert operations . . . like sabotaging enemy equipment.

Jeremy's father emerged from the house. He was holding a can of beer, and looked unhappy. "There you are. Where have you been, boy?" His voice was husky and rough, the result of smoking too many cigarettes.

"I . . . I lost rack of time," Jeremy stammered. He looked at his approaching father with a frightened expression.

"You lost rack of time." His old man set the beer can down on the picnic table with a loud thunk. "How many times do I have to tell you? Your chores come first, then you can waste time on foolishness."

"I . . . I'm sorry," Jeremy said. "It won't happen again."

"That's what you keep telling me. Now, get in the shed."

"No, Dad. I won't do it again, I promise. Just give me another chance," Jeremy pleaded.

"I'm done giving you chances. I've given you enough chances. Now, get in the shed. The longer you wait, the worse it will be."

"Dad, no, please!"

"In the shed, now." The man grabbed the boy by the arm, and roughly guided him toward the shed. He gave a harsh shove, and Jeremy nearly stumbled forward onto his face.

Tobias watched silently as the tall, ruggedly built man shoved his teenaged son inside the shed, slamming the door shut behind them. Immediately, he could hear the sounds of Jeremy begging for forgiveness and weeping from within. He need to get a closer look.

The little winged man left the cover of the tree, and quickly flew around to the back of the shed. Peering in through a rear window, he saw that the large shed was filled with hand tools and garden equipment, with a work bench on one side by itself. The man had removed his belt, and was about to strike his son with it.

"This is for your own good," he said.

Tobias watched in utter horror as the man started lashing at the boy with the belt. He struck the boy on the butt through his faded blue jeans. He struck him so hard that he would have felt it through several layers of clothing. The boy uttered one cry of pain after another. The sounds were pitiful, and Tobias really felt sorry for him. He looked so frightened and helpless, his lengthy dark brown hair covering his moist brown eyes. Tears streamed down his face.

Tobias had to act quickly. Seeing a stone on the ground nearby, he swooped down to retrieve it. Taking to the air again, he took aim a the window, and tossed the rock as hard as he could. The stone smashed through the window, glass shattering and spraying everywhere.

All activity within abruptly ceased. "What the . . ." he heard the man yell.

Tobias waited. The man rushed to the broken window, and his eyes went wide as his gaze met Tobias. Angry, Tobias flew inside and smashed into the man, sending him crashing into the work bench. Tools and half-finished projects scattered everywhere, and the man scrambled to right himself.

Tobias grabbed the belt. Hovering in the air, he lashed at the man once, twice, three times, catching him in the chest, on the shoulder, and the third time in his face.

"How does that feel?" Tobias asked irately when he was finished. "Huh? Do you like it? Does it feel good?" He hovered in midair, glaring down at the man with his amber eyes as his tail wrapped around the man's neck. The man struggled to remove the gradually tightening tail to no avail. The harder he tried, the tighter it was. The tail began restricting air flow, and the man's face was changing color. He tried to speak, but the only thing that came out was a raspy, gurgling sound. The man stared up at him with a mix of fear and wonder in his face.

"Tobias, what are you doing?" Jeremy asked, alarmed. He had recovered himself, and was watching intently from a distance.

"Teaching him a lesson. Don't worry, I won't kill him."

"Now, you listen up, and listen good," Tobias said. "If you ever harm the boy again, it will be the last time . . . understand?"

The man nodded. Tobias loosened his grip, and the man collapsed to the floor in a heap, desperately trying to catch his breath.

"Are you all right, Jeremy?" Tobias asked, turning to the boy. Jeremy nodded, not knowing what to make of the whole ordeal, thoroughly grateful for Tobias's intervention.

"Thank you, Tobias," Jeremy said. He was still standing completely still, unable or unwilling to move.

"If he ever touches you again, you just let me know," Tobias said. "I'll come back, and he'll be sorry, I promise you." Turning back to glare at the boy's father, he added, "You got that, creep?"

"Who are you?" The man croaked, swallowing. "What the hell are you?"

"A friend of Jeremy's, and an enemy of yours," Tobias replied tersely.

Tobias turned back to Jeremy. He reached in a pocket, and retrieved a small device. It was emerald green, and looked like a gem, but it was actually a piece of alien technology. "Here, take this. Keep it in a safe place. If you ever need help again, rub it and call my name. I'll be here shortly thereafter. Okay?"

"Okay."

"And as for you," he said as he scowled at the boy's father, "you can do your own chores. Jeremy and I are going for a walk."

The man said nothing. His mouth opened, but he couldn't find his vocal chords. He merely stared at Tobias warily.

"Come on, Jeremy . . . to heck with the chores. Maybe your old man will appreciate you more if he has to do his own work for awhile." With one final look at the boy's father, who was finally gathering himself, getting back to his feet, he said, "Remember, one scratch on the boy, and you will pay with your life." That said, he left the shed.

"I don't know if I should go with you," Jeremy said as he joined Tobias outside. "He's going to be mad as hell over this."

"And if he touches you, I'll be back. All you have to do is rub the gem, and call my name. My transport module will have me here in little more than a minute."

"Son." The boy's father emerged from the shed, visibly shaken by the ordeal. "I'm sorry. I'll never raise a hand to you again."

"How many times have I heard that before, Dad?" Jeremy asked, emboldened by Tobias at his side.

"I know. I was wrong. A boy your age needs time to unwind, have fun, what with school and all. You can do your chores later."

"You'll do them yourself," Tobias snapped. "At least for now. Jeremy and I are going for a walk. He's going to teach me about your planet."

"My planet?" The man's eyes widened. He looked older than he was, haggard, with lines and pock marks on his face. His hair was nearly entirely gray, leaving very little evidence that he once had blond hair. He hadn't shaved in days. He had the look of a man who didn't take care of himself. He looked like a bum.

"Tobias is from a planet called Celtica, Dad. He and his friends are lost in space. They're explorers, and they go on all sorts of adventures." His explanation was spoken as if people heard such things every day. His father stared at them both as for a long while, unable to think of anything to say.

"So long," Tobias said. "I'll have him home in a couple of hours." Turning his attention to Jeremy, he said, "Let's go, kid. Lead the way and show me something."

The boy's father watched them leave, his son on foot and Tobias flying at head height. He stared after them until they were nearly out of sight in the field behind the house. Bewildered, he made his way back to the house.

He never treated his son badly again.

CHAPTER THIRTEEN

T he Solar Flare was a triangular shaped space craft. It was white with black trim; part flying machine, part living entity. It was the most sophisticated, technologically advanced space shop known to exist. It is very old, having been handed down from generation to generation in Evan Starkweather's bloodline. The details of how the ship was created is a mystery, although it is known that Evan's father and grandfather had a lot to do with it. It is believed that a number of uncles participated as well.

The Solar Flare had been traveling through space for an unknown period of time when it stumbled upon the Earth. The guidance system failed at some point in time, unbeknownst to Evan and his crew, who were in suspended animation. The Solar Flare should have awakened Evan and the others automatically when the trouble occurred, but the space craft's artificial intelligence was only partially functioning, the cause being unknown. The ship dispatched the transport module to retrieve help. The big silver bell happened to be first seen by Ryan Bettencourt. It had been a random chance encounter.

At the very front of the space ship, at one of the three points of the triangle, was the control room. There was a set of double doors at the rear of the control room that led to a main corridor. To the left was what was called the left wing; this was where the galley, recreation area, living room, and crew quarters were located. On the opposite side of the main corridor was the right wing, where the research labs, main library, infirmary, and storage bays were located. At the end of the main corridor was the engine room. There was a shallow lower deck in the belly of the space ship, and this is where food storage, replacement parts, electrical and plumbing, and miscellaneous storage compartments were located, as well as a maximum security holding cell. Fortunately, this holding cell, which would be used for intruders and other hostile visitors, has seldom had to be used.

It was the middle of the night, Solar Flare time, when the long dormant consciousness of the ship reawakened. Being telepathic, it immediately called out to Autumn.

Autumn awakened from a sound sleep. Her eyes opened, and she listened with held breath. The ship called her name again. She heard its voice in her mind. It was a very neutral sounding voice, not quite male, not quite female. It was a distinct voice, one that could not be mistaken. Autumn heard it a third time, and she sat up in bed.

"Solar Flare? Is that you, or am I dreaming?" She whispered.

"Yes, it is I."

"What happened to you? I haven't been able to contact you telepathically. It's like you were dead."

"I wasn't dead, merely incapacitated."

"What happened?"

"I do not entirely know," Solar Flare began. "My memories of the ordeal are fragmentary. Strangers boarded me while you and the others were in hibernation. They tried to breach my security systems, but were not entirely successful. They studied me for awhile, then sabotaged some of my systems. My self regeneration capabilities were able to repair most of the damage."

"Solar Flare, that's very unsettling news," Autumn said, again speaking aloud rather than telepathically. "I'd better tell Evan." Then, she shook her husband, who was sound asleep beside her.

"Evan . . . Evan, wake up."

"Mm . . ." Evan mumbled as he awakened, turning to look at his wife with a frown. "What's the matter?" He asked as he stared at her, blinking as he tried to shake off his sleep.

"The Solar Flare is alive," Autumn said. "It just contacted me telepathically. Evan, the ship told me some disturbing news."

"What is it?" Evan waited patiently for her to continue, his upper body now propped up on his elbows and forearms.

"While were in suspended animation, invaders came aboard the ship. They studied the Solar Flare, then sabotaged certain systems. That's the reason we haven't been able to communicate with it."

"Trevor and I will review the security tapes in the morning," Evan said. He was fully awake now because of the troubling news. "Just the fact the invaders were able to get on board is very disconcerting." He frowned, adding, "I wonder if they were someone that we know of."

"What do you mean?" Autumn asked.

"Well, we have made a few enemies along the way," Evan said. "Enemies that know a little bit about Celtica's technology."

Autumn looked deeply concerned.

"Don't worry, darling," Evan said, smiling. "Anyone who threatens us will be up against a formidable opponent. We've faced some of the most dangerous creatures in the galaxy, don't forget." He touched her bare knee, adding, "We'll be all right. Besides, we're hundreds of lights years from home. There's nothing out here except little old Earth."

"Darn. I was beginning to think we were about to embark on a dangerous adventure," Autumn joked, and they both laughed.

"Since you woke me up, and it's nearly time to get up, anyway . . . ." Evan began, leaving his statement unfinished as he smiled mischievously.

"Are you thinking what I think you're thinking?" Autumn asked, moving closer, snuggling up to him.

"You're telepathic . . . you tell me."

"I don't need telepathy to know." Autumn said, taking him into her embrace and holding him tight. Evan likewise held her. She reached for his lips with hers, and they kissed. She wrapped a leg around his, and kissed him more passionately. One kiss led to another, and then another. Soon, they were engaged in other, more intimate things.

There was no more talk of enemy intruders or saboteurs for the time being.

CHAPTER FOURTEEN

The galley was a rectangular room, the length of it running from its entrance to the rear wall. A long rectangular table with high-backed chairs was in the center, running from the rear wall outward. To the left of the table were the food preparation apparatus and a counter with a number of appliances of alien deign. To the right of the table was the food storage equipment, along with cabinets and more counter space. Like much of the rest of the ship, there were blue walls, a black floor, and w a white ceiling. Everything else was mostly done in shades of grey and black, with the exception of the shiny silver appliances. Everything was polished to a shine, and everything looked and smelled clean. The galley reminded Braden of what a human kitchen might look like two hundred years from now.

Braden and Stella were in the galley at four o'clock in the morning, Solar Flare time. The planet Celtica had a twenty-six hour day, as opposed to earth's twenty-four. Since few worlds had the same rotation time, the Solar Flare crew used Celtica time for the ships' chronometers.

Stella was treating Braden to a Celtican snack. It wasn't all that different from chocolate cake and vanilla ice cream, although the look, taste, and texture wasn't quite the same. Braden found it to be rather good. They washed it down with Celtican red wine. The wine was tasty but stronger than human wine, he thought. He was feeling lightheaded by the time he drained his glass.

"So, what do you think of the Solar Flare so far?" Stella asked.

"It's quite unlike anything I've ever seen before. In fact, it's unlike anything any human has ever seen before. I found that botanical garden, especially, quite interesting." *Even though it was rather unnerving,* he added in his thoughts.

"I'm glad to hear you say that." Stella smiled, then quickly sobered as she searched for the right words to say. "I was wondering . . . since you have no job and stuff, and since you find your life boring, would you . . . well, what would you think about traveling to other stars, going on adventures with me? Uh, with us?" She quickly amended. She didn't want him to know she was more than a little interested in him.

"Huh? You mean it? I mean . . . me, travel with you guys?" He thought about that for a moment. "I don't know. It would be kind of weird. No human had ever joined aliens on space voyages before."

"So, be the first."

"I don't know, Stella. I mean, once you guys leave, you're never coming back, right? I'd never see my family again. I think I'd get homesick."

"I haven't seen home in a long time, Braden. I miss it sometimes. But, there's something special about a life of adventure. It's like nothing else . . . it's exciting. Trust me, once you got used to it, you'd never want to give it up."

"But, it's a lonely life, isn't it? I mean, Evan and Autumn have each other, but you, Trevor, and Tobias have no one. You said yourself it can be lonely at times."

"It can be," Stella said with a nod. "But, we're never really alone. We have each other . . . we're a family."

"But, a companion," Braden said, "like Evan and Autumn."

"People have come and gone," Stella said with a shrug. "Maybe I just haven't found that special one, yet. It doesn't matter. Lonely or not, I wouldn't give up my life."

"I don't know if I could do it, Stella."

"It's not like you have to decide today. We're not going anywhere for awhile. The ship needs repairs, and we don't even know where we are. We're stuck here for the time being. It's just something for you to think about. It's a great life."

"This was delicious," Braden said, changing the subject. Although, in the back of his mind he was indeed thinking about her proposal. His life situation at present was going nowhere.

"And the wine," he added as he tried to get off his chair. He stumbled and lost his balance in the process, nearly falling over as he swayed on his feet. Stella rushed to his side, helping to steady him. She moved so quickly

Braden hadn't seen her move. *It must be an affect of this Celtican wine,* he mused.

"Are you all right, Braden?"

"Yeah, I'm okay." He laughed, looking at her sheepishly. Their faces were only inches apart. Something about the way she was looking at him made him feel funny. His stomach knotted, and his pulse quickened. He tensed.

"Your tense, Braden. Relax." She turned him gently around to face her, then she put her arms around him, holding him close. Their bodies touched from chest to waist. Strangely, Braden had grown calm. It had to do with the power of Stella's touch.

"It . . . ah . . . I think it might be the wine," Braden stammered, laughing softly. Ordinarily, he'd be embarrassed. He wasn't.

"It's okay," Stella said. "Don't worry about it."

"I'm not worried," Braden's speech was a little slurred, and he felt weird. He wasn't sure if it was the wine or something to do with Stella.

"Good." Stella leaned closer, and gave Braden a kiss on the lips. It was a soft, subtle kiss; the kind shared between two attracted people who just met. "Hey, you look exhausted, Braden. Why don't I show you to the guest room? You can sleep for awhile."

"Sounds good," Braden said. He was feeling tipsy now, and his tongue was clumsy when he spoke. It had to be the alien wine, he thought.

Stella helped him to the guest room, and then into bed. She turned out the light, and closed the door as she left the room. Braden was asleep within seconds, and was out for several hours.

CHAPTER FIFTEEN

Tobias took Jeremy back home later that day. Then, he wandered off into the neighborhood. He ended up in someone's garden, and was eating ripe red tomatoes. The homeowner ventured out after dinner in order to weed and water the garden. To his dismay, Tobias was sitting in the center of the garden, sampling more of the vegetables. Tobias finally realized he was being watched, and saw the middle-aged man staring at him from a distance with an amazed expression on his face. He didn't know what to make of Tobias, and so he stood there for a rather long time, simply watching the little winged man.

"Hello," Tobias said. "I was hungry. I hope you don't mind that I ate some of your vegetables."

"What in hell are you?" The man asked.

"My name is Tobias. I'm from the planet Celtica."

"Holy crap" the man stated in awe. "I must be seeing things." He closed his eyes, then opened them again. Tobias was still there.

"Nope, you're not," Tobias said. "I'm quite real." He stood, giving the man a better view of his eighteen inch, fifteen pound frame. His wings were big enough to wrap himself in. He stared at the man with piercing amber eyes, with a half-eaten tomato in one hand, and a fist full of green beans in the other.

At first, the man stared incredulously, not knowing what to do. Then, a slow anger began to boil in him as he looked around and saw that several plants had been picked nearly clean. Tobias hadn't merely snacked; he'd had himself a feast.

"Look what you've done to my garden! You little . . . thing! You're going to pay dearly for this.

The man stomped toward Tobias. Tobias's amber eyes went wide, and then he went into motion. The man literally dove at the little winged man; but, Tobias was too quick. He scampered toward some bushes at the perimeter of the man's property. The man landed on the ground with a grunt.

"You little . . ." The man, who was short, pudgy, and definitely out of shape, gathered himself as he got to his knees, huffing and puffing. Finally, he managed to get back to his feet. Eyes narrowed in determination, he went after Tobias in the bush where he was hiding.

"You come out of there, you little garden assassin," he growled, shaking the bush in an attempt to get Tobias to emerge from the bush. Tobias did, only to fly up at the man's face, slamming into him like a cannonball. The man keeled over backward, pin wheeling in an attempt to remain upright. He failed. Tobias laughed as he flew up into a nearby tree. He watched from where he hid, his green skin and wings camouflaging him perfectly.

Refusing to give up, the man retrieved a garden hoe, and proceeded to the tree. He scowled as he shoved the hoe into the tree to try and extract Tobias. The little winged man simply climbed higher and out of reach. The man could see his amber eyes staring down at him. They glowed like those of a cat.

"What the hell are you?" The man mumbled to himself, repeating the question as if the little winged man's explanation didn't suffice. He certainly didn't believe the creature was from some alien planet . . . he didn't even believe in aliens.

Determination unwavering, the man started to climb the tree. It probably wasn't the wisest decision he ever made, being so out of shape from an unhealthy diet, not enough exercise, and too many cigarettes. But, up the tree he went, huffing and puffing. Tobias watched from above with little more than casual interest.

The man was nearly halfway up the tree when he lost his footing. He slipped and ended up tangled in branches, arms and legs twisted in different directions. Tobias found this to be very amusing. He tossed his head back in laughter. His laughing came to an abrupt halt, however, when he felt a tug on his tail. The man held it firmly in his grip.

"Hey, let go!" Tobias yelled. "That hurts!"

"I've got you now, you little winged imp," the man growled. He pulled on Tobias's tail in an attempt to bring him down. Tobias squealed in pain, using both hands to try and yank his tail free.

"I'll teach you to ravage a person's garden, you little sucker."

"What do you want with a garden, anyway?" Tobias asked angrily, still trying to free his tail from the man's relentless grip. "You obviously don't eat vegetables, or you wouldn't be so fat."

"I don't know what you are or where you came from," the man scoffed, "but we'll see if you're still a funny guy once I'm done with you." He yanked hard on Tobias's tail. Tobias cried out in agony.

Tobias went into full self-preservation mode. With his claws extended, he lunged at the man, and slashed his face. Now it was the other guy's turn to cry out in agony. He instinctively let go of Tobias's tail in order to cover his face with his hands. He was bleeding, and his flesh stung.

Tobias fled the tree, and landed on the ground. Neighbors had come out of their homes to investigate upon hearing the sounds of the struggle. They were gawking over fences or standing on their patios. The man's wife and two teenaged children also came outside to investigate. They, along with their neighbors, stared at Tobias in utter wonder. At first, everyone thought he was some kind of small animal. Upon closer inspection, however, they all realized that he wasn't an animal, and in fact was not of this world.

The man was still moaning and groaning, crying almost as he finally emerged from the tree. His face was a bloody mess, and he looked as though he might pass out. He was breathing heavily, and his face was ashen.

"Max!" The man's wife cried as she hurried over to where he was.

"Dad, what happened to you?" His son asked. His daughter started crying, keeping herself at a safe distance.

"That little winged . . . thing! He attacked me! Oh, I'd better sit down." His wife led him to the nearby picnic table.

"He came after me," Tobias stated angrily. "I acted in self-defense."

The man's wife and daughter gasped.

"It talks!" The son exclaimed, eyes wide.

Mobile phones came out, and several of the neighbors began taking pictures and video of the strange winged creature in their neighbor's back yard. The couple's son did the same with his phone, including footage of his father's bloody face. There were deep scratches on both sides of his face, and blood trailed down his cheeks and onto his gardening clothes.

"Get that . . . that thing!" His mother ordered, glaring at Tobias yet too afraid to do it herself. Her son went after Tobias, but Tobias flew off before he could even get close. The little winged man soared high into the sky, and soon he was out of sight.

The neighborhood was buzzing with gossip and speculation for the remainder of the evening, and beyond. It would mark the beginning of major trouble for Tobias and the others as news of the incident began to spread; and, the end of their ability to mingle with humans in total anonymity.

CHAPTER SIXTEEN

Ryan Bettencourt parked in the parking spot reserved for him in the parking lot behind his real estate business. He climbed out his sleek black luxury car, closed the door, and secured the lock. Then, with his briefcase in his left hand and his keys in the other, he proceeded to the back entrance of the building.

He was early today. Breakfast hadn't gone well due to the continuing friction between his wife and himself, so he figured there was nothing better to do that to head to work early. Heather, his office manager and personal secretary, was usually the first to arrive. She would unlock, open window blinds, and make a pot of coffee. She wasn't due in for another twenty minutes, so today, he would be doing those things.

Ryan went about preparing for business, then proceeded to his office. He opened the door, walked in, and closed the door behind him. After opening his window blinds, he then headed for his desk. He cried out when he discovered Autumn sitting in his chair. He froze, not knowing what to do.

"Hello, Ryan," Autumn said pleasantly, looking amused by his confounded state.

"What are you doing here?" He finally managed.

"I stopped by for a visit."

"How did you get in?"

"Oh, it was quite easy. You humans need to improve your security measures."

"The door was locked, and the security was on," Ryan said.

"I picked the lock with this." She held up a small, silver, pencil shaped device. "It also knocked out your security system. Neat, huh?"

"I demand to know the meaning of this. In human society, there are certain protocols for paying visits. Breaking and entering isn't one of them."

"Oh." Autumn pretended looking perplexed. "What should have I done?"

"Well, since this is my place of business," Ryan began, "the proper thing to do would be to make an appointment."

"I see." Autumn smiled wickedly.

"And that is my chair," he continued tersely, regaining some of his composure.

"Today it's mine." Autumn sneered. "Pretend I'm the proprietor, and you're the customer. See? I've put on a fancy suit for the occasion. Please, do sit down." She gestured to the two chairs situated before the desk. It was a huge desk, and the chair behind it was big, plush black leather. Autumn's five foot, one-hundred pound frame looked tiny in it.

"I demand to know the meaning of this," Ryan said as he looked Autumn over. She was dressed in a green business suit with a skirt that came to the knees, and a frilly white blouse beneath the jacket. She wore dark green pumps on her feet with open toes and a single strap that wrapped around her heel. Her attire went good with her pale skin, long red hair, and green eyes.

"There you go with the demands again," She said with a touch of impatience. "Don't you get it, yet? You are in no position to demand anything. I'm in charge here. Now, sit your ass down in one of those chairs before the desk."

"You will get out of my chair, and *you* will sit in one of these chairs," he stated defiantly.

Autumn's expression clouded over. She stared at Ryan, and, with nothing more than the sheer will of her mind, he found it difficult to breathe. The air thickened, and there seemed to be too little of it. Ryan dropped his briefcase, and immediately grabbed at his throat with both hands.

"I don't like your tone, Ryan," Autumn said. "I don't think you realize who you're dealing with. Now, I strongly suggest you change your attitude, mister." She sat there watching him struggling to breath with a sinister grin on her face.

Ryan's face changed colors, and he fell to his knees. The edges of his vision were going grey, and he felt lightheaded. He looked at Autumn imploringly, his expression one of utter fear, his eyes bulging.

"Had enough" Autumn asked.

Ryan nodded frantically, about to lose consciousness at any moment. Autumn released her hold on him, and he was able to breathe again.

"Please take one of the chairs, Ryan, before I lose my patience again. Next time, I may not be so lenient."

"What do you want?" Ryan asked as he did as he was told. It felt weird sitting on the opposite side of the desk. He was just glad to be breathing again.

"I want to talk," Autumn replied as if the answer should have been obvious. "Why else does someone stop by for a visit?"

"Well, what do you want?" Ryan asked. He was still visibly shaken by the ordeal.

"Two things," Autumn responded. "First, I want to let you know that your situation with your wife will be resolved soon."

Ryan's mood brightened, at least a little. "And, the second?"

"I need to place a locator chip in you."

"A locator chip?" Ryan asked warily.

"We need to be able to find you when we want to. The locator chip will enable us to do that."

"And, if I refuse?"

"Then, you can kiss your wife goodbye." Autumn said with a shrug. "It makes no difference to me."

"You're a little witch." Ryan said.

"Is that a no?"

"No, I'll cooperate, since I'm left with little choice."

"I thought you might say that." Autumn smiled. "Roll up your sleeves." A small, silver, cylindrical device appeared in her open palm. It had a pointed tip, and a red button on the side of it.

Ryan eyed the device in her hand warily as he pushed up the sleeve of his grey suit jacket, then unbuttoned the cuff of his white shirt in order to roll up the sleeve.

"Is this going to hurt?" He asked.

"Is this going to hurt?" Autumn repeated in a mocking tone. Then, with an air of impatience, added, "Ryan, stop acting like a wimp. Be a man."

Ryan stretched his bare arm across the desk without further comment. Autumn injected the locator chip in the meaty part of his arm, about halfway between his wrist and elbow. Then the implement she'd used disappeared before his eyes. He was utterly astounded. He sat back and stared at Autumn incredulously as he absently rolled down his sleeve, buttoned the cuff, and smoothed out his suit jacket.

"Would you have killed me?" He asked after a lengthy silence.

"Of course not," Autumn replied as if he was being silly. "I'm not a killer, Ryan. I just felt a demonstration of my power was in order. You were getting cocky . . . I wanted you to know who had the upper hand."

There was a knock at the door. "Ryan, your nine o'clock appointment is here," Heather said. "Shall I send them in?"

Ryan looked at Autumn questioningly. "Well?" He asked.

Autumn remained silent. Her expression had changed. Instead of looking smug and amused, she now appeared worried. She was staring at Ryan, but saying nothing.

"Autumn?" He prompted. "I have customers waiting."

"You go ahead and tend to your business," Autumn said, her entire demeanor changed. She stood, adding, "Something's come up. I need to get to the Solar Flare."

"What is it?" Ryan asked as he likewise stood, curious as to what the trouble was. Something was obviously bothering her.

"I'd rather not get into it now," Autumn replied as she rushed past him and toward the door. Ryan watched as she opened the door and entered the main office, then followed.

Heather was standing near the door where clients entered with a young couple who were looking to buy a house. Heather eyed Autumn with a puzzled expression as the petite redhead made her way toward the rear door. She then looked at Ryan, who shrugged and said, "I'll be right back," he told the customers with a smile as he followed Autumn out.

When they arrived outside, the big silver bell was standing ready to take Autumn back to the space ship. The door was open, and Autumn made a beeline toward it, walking briskly. Ryan hurried after her.

"Wait up," he said, huffing and puffing as he came to a stop just outside the open door. Autumn turned around to face him, standing in the threshold.

"What?" She asked impatiently.

"What's wrong?" Ryan asked. "I don't have to be telepathic like you to know something's the matter."

"I told you I'll talk to you later," Autumn said. "I have pressing matters to tend to aboard the ship." Ryan opened his mouth to speak, but she continued, "When you go home tonight, things will be different. Your marriage will be as it once was. Now, I have important things to do."

"But, when will I . . ."

She cut him off. "Bye, Ryan."

Autumn ducked inside. The door closed, and the big silver bell disappeared in a whisper of sound.

CHAPTER SEVENTEEN

"Take a look at this," Trevor said as everyone gathered around him at his console in the control room. The rectangular viewing screen on the wall above his control panel displayed the incident with Tobias. Someone had uploaded images of Tobias and the badly injured man onto the internet.

"Look at that guy's face," Braden exclaimed.

"He's a mess," Stella added.

"Tobias was defending himself," Autumn said. "I'm sure of it."

"I'm inclined to agree with you," Evan said. "But, we didn't actually see what happened . . . only the results."

"Where *is* Tobias?" Stella asked.

"Come to think of it, I haven't seen him since he left yesterday afternoon," Autumn said.

"Trevor, he was working with you yesterday," Evan began. "Did he say where he was going?"

"No. I found him sleeping on the job, and when I woke him, he complained about being worked too hard. He stormed off, and I haven't seen him since."

Evan looked at the images on the screen. The video had gone viral, and people were posting it on their social networking profiles.

"I don't like this," Autumn said.

"There's more." Trevor switched to a news station. The same footage was playing to the accompaniment of a female reporter's voice. Stills were shown of the injured man, as well as Tobias. When the report was finished, the program switched back to the news desk. A man and a woman were speculating as what Tobias could be.

"This is really bad," Evan said. "The entire planet is seeing this."

"I advised against allowing him to go to the planet's surface unaccompanied," Trevor said.

"And, I gave strict orders that he was not to go to the planet's surface alone," Evan added.

"It's not like he hasn't disobeyed orders before," Autumn said.

Evan shook his head, and sighed. "We'd better find him before he gets himself in even more trouble."

Trevor met his gaze, nodding in agreement. "Not to mention the trouble he's causing us," he added.

Evan went over to the main controls, and switched on the communication system. "Solar Flare to Tobias . . . check in, please."

There was no response. "Solar Flare to Tobias . . . this is Evan, please respond."

"He's not answering," Stella stated needlessly.

"Maybe he can't answer," Autumn said.

Evan tried once more, speaking sternly. "Tobias, if you can hear me, respond, please . . . that's an order." His only response was snowy static.

"He's in trouble," Autumn stated softly.

"You'd better believe it," Trevor grumbled. "When I get my hands on him . . ."

"No, I mean he's really in trouble," Autumn interjected. "I can sense it."

Evan and the others looked at her with deep concern, even their guest, who wasn't yet up to sped on Autumn's telepathic and psychic abilities.

"I hate it when you say that," Evan said.

"Me, too," Stella added.

"So, what are we going to do?" Trevor asked. The tall, ruggedly built black man was ready for action. His black hair flowed to his shoulders, and his brown eyes were steely determination.

"We'll find him with his locator chip," Evan said. "We'll all go down. We may need every member of the team."

Trevor eyed Braden, then looked back at Evan. "What about our guest?"

"He can stay with me," Stella said.

"That may not be a good idea," Trevor objected.

"If he's going to be one of our human contacts," Stella continued, "he may as well get a taste of what our lives are like."

"An exchange of cultures. I get it," Evan stated with a wave of the hand. Then, to Braden, he said, "You remain with Stella at all times, you understand?"

"Yes, sir," Braden replied shyly.

"And, you will do as she says," Evan added.

"I understand, sir."

"Evan will do, Braden. I'm not big on formalities."

Braden nodded. "Okay."

"Okay, then," Evan continued. "Let's go."

They stepped into the transport capsule, and went down to the surface in search of Tobias.

CHAPTER EIGHTEEN

The transport capsule materialized in a wooded area behind an elementary school. The door opened, and they all stepped out. Evan then sent the vehicle back to the space ship until needed.

Evan was wearing blue jeans and a blue sweatshirt, with blue and white running shoes. Autumn was also in jeans, with a green top and running shoes. Trevor wore black jeans, a black short sleeved shirt, and hiking boots. Stella was also in black, foregoing her usual dress or skirt for a pair of black jeans. Braden was in blue jeans, a gray sweatshirt, and matching hiking boots. They wanted to dress for maximum maneuverability in case they had to run or fight. They also wanted to dress like humans so they could blend in with the locals.

"Tobias is close by," Evan said, studying the screen of his mobile device.

"I can sense his presence," Autumn said.

"This way." Evan led the others to the edge of the woods, where they all peered out into a playground. It was recess time, and dozens of children were at play. They watched the children for a time, scanning the grounds for signs of Tobias.

"Look over there!" Autumn said excitedly. She pointed toward a swing set.

Tobias was at the top of the attached slide, about to make his way down. Several children cheered him on, and down he went. When he got to the bottom, he flew back to the top rather than using the ladder.

"He's playing with the children," Stella stated cheerfully. "How sweet."

"I can understand the children taking a liking to him," Evan said. "The adults, though, are another matter, especially considering how widespread the news is about what he did."

"Perhaps they haven't noticed him yet," Trevor suggested.

They continued to observe as Tobias continued to entertain the children. He flew up the air, circled around, and dove downward again, going around and around at eye level with them. He did several stunts in the air to a chorus of cheers, excited squeals, and laughter. As for Tobias, he thoroughly enjoyed the attention.

All this commotion managed to get the attention of the adults at last. Two teachers who had been talking together looked over, their eyes going wide as their minds struggled to accept what they saw. A third teacher also took notice, and hurried over to the other two. The trio of educators spoke in a huddle, their gazes remaining focused on Tobias and the large gathering around him.

"Uh oh . . . I think someone just noticed," Stella said.

"And now, she's talking to someone else," Evan added.

A third adult joined the other two, and all three were making their way over to Tobias and his little band of playmates.

"This isn't good," Autumn said. "I have a feeling things are going to get ugly."

"The voice of gloom and doom." Evan gave his wife a little ribbing even though he knew she'd be right. They exchanged smiles, and Autumn made a face at him.

Trevor jabbed Evan with an elbow. "Look. They're breaking it up."

The adults cried out and made loud noises at Tobias, like one might do to scare off an animal. Tobias merely watched from his perch at the top of the slide as the teachers corralled the children and brought them back inside. Several youngsters glanced back at Tobias along the way. There were groans of protest as their fun was brought to an end, and none of them looked happy about it.

"But, he's friendly," one of the children could be heard saying. "He wouldn't hurt us."

"He only wanted to play," stated another.

The clamor abruptly ceased when all of the schoolchildren were back indoors, and the doors were secured. The entire school was locked down while school officials called the authorities.

"Well, the playground is empty except for Tobias," Stella said.

"We'd better act quickly," Autumn warned.

"Let's go get him," Evan said.

"Yes, let's go get the little pain in the ass before he causes us more trouble," Trevor added.

Evan led the way, and the others followed. They proceeded to where Tobias was, still sitting at the top of the slide and looking disappointed.

"There you are," Evan said as they came approached. "Do you realize how much trouble you caused? You're all over the news, as well as the internet."

"Yeah, good job, you little winged troublemaker," Trevor scolded.

"Hey, that wasn't my fault," Tobias countered angrily. "If he'd have just let me leave, none of that would have happened. I acted in self-defense."

"Maybe so," Evan said. "Nevertheless, our anonymity in this society has been compromised. Now, let's get out of here . . . Autumn senses trouble."

"Why should I leave?" Tobias asked. "Why did they have to bring the children inside? We were all having fun."

"They brought them inside because a man's mutilated face is all over the news," Trevor grumbled. "And, they know you are the cause."

"But I didn't mean to do it! And, I wouldn't hurt the children."

"We know that," Evan said, "but they don't. Now, let's go."

"But . . . that's not fair!" Tobias complained, sounding like a child who'd just been told it was time to come in and get ready for bed.

"I'm not going back to the ship, Tobias snapped. "I'm tired of him pushing me around, working me to death." He pointed at Trevor.

There came the sound of sirens as police cars made their way through the busy streets, getting other motorists to pull over and clear the way for them. They were getting closer, and quickly.

"You hear those sirens?" Evan asked. "We can discuss your complaints later," Evan said. "Right now, we have to get out of here before the authorities arrive."

"They're here," Autumn said, sensing their approach.

"Quickly, let's get back in the woods," Evan ordered, taking the lead as the others followed. Everyone, that is, except Tobias; he stubbornly remained where he was, perched atop the playground equipment.

"Tobias, let's go," Evan barked when they reached the edge of the woods, realizing he hadn't joined them.

"If you don't move your ass, we'll leave you to the human authorities," Trevor barked impatiently.

Tobias looked back. Uniformed policemen were rounding the corner, entering the rear of the property where the playground was. He looked back at his friends. Finally, he decided to follow.

It was to late. A number of uniformed police officers rounded the corner, accompanied by men in suits. They spotted Tobias almost right away as the little winged man took to the air. There was a quick reaction by one of the suits, and then Tobias cried out. He faltered, and then fell to the ground on a motionless heap. He'd been hit with a tranquilizer dart.

The men in suits gathered around Tobias. Two of them crouched beside the little winged man, and one of them rolled him onto his back while the others observed with curious interest. The uniformed cops came closer, likewise looking on with great interest.

Nobody seemed to notice Evan and the others, who were watching events unfold from the security of the nearby woods. Evan and Trevor were standing with weapons drawn, but did not take aim, at least not for the moment. Autumn, Stella, and Braden were gathered together not far away. No one would make a move until Evan gave an order. Each of them was ready.

A dark blue, unmarked van emerged on the scene, and came to a stop near the gathering on the playground. The driver remained behind the wheel, and waited patiently with the engine running.

One of the suits went to the van and removed a cage large enough for Tobias with room to spare. He brought it to where the little winged man lay, and set it on the ground. Another man stuffed Tobias in the cage, and secured the door.

"They're putting him in a cage," Autumn incredulously.

"Like he's some kind of animal," Stella sated in awe.

"They're probably taking him somewhere so they can study him," Braden said. "No human has ever seen anything like Tobias before." He shook his head, adding, "They'll do all sorts of experiments on him. They may even kill him so they can dissect him. It's believed that there are research facilities for such things."

"Would you please elaborate on that?" Evan asked.

"We've been fascinated with extraterrestrial life for generations," Braden explained. "We've devoted countless resources to the discovery and study of extraterrestrial life . . . like the S.E.T.I. Institute and Berkely Astronomy Laboratory; an array of forty-two radio telescopes that continually search for intelligent life elsewhere in the universe.

"Really?" Evan's eyebrows rose, and he seemed quite fascinated.

"There's also supposedly a place in Arizona where they've collected numerous alien artifacts," Braden continued. "Pieces of crashed UFO's, bits of alien technology, and so on. I'm telling you, we humans are obsessed with that stuff. Your friend is very big trouble."

"They've put him in the van," Stella stated anxiously.

"Evan, we've got to do something," Autumn said. "While you two are having this inane conversation, those people are taking Tobias away."

"I'm open to suggestions," Evan said.

"We could fire upon them," Trevor suggested. "Take a couple of them out . . . that should get their attention."

"Your superior weaponry would definitely give you the element of surprise," Braden said.

"They're armed," Evan pointed out. "I'm not interested in engaging in a gun battle."

"We're protected by trees, and they're out in the open," Trevor said. "The only thing they're likely to do is run for cover."

"Maybe not," Braden said. They all looked at him, and he added, "Your weapons will take them by surprise. They'll freeze, not sure of what to do at first. Those few seconds may be all you need."

"The boy may be right," Trevor commented. "With the element of surprise, we could rush them with weapons drawn. We could force a surrender."

"What if Braden is wrong, and they react like the trained officers that they are?" Evan asked, shaking his head. "If we end up in a fight, someone may either get hurt or killed. So far, all they've seen is Tobias. He's the one all over the news, and he's the one who can't blend in with humans. We've still got our anonymity . . . we can use that to our advantage."

"Well, Evan, what are we going to do, then?" Autumn asked.

"We go back to the ship, and wait. We can track Tobias via his locator chip. We'll wait until he gets to his destination, then we'll act."

"And, that's better than acting now? How, exactly?" Autumn asked.

"The trip will allow us to plan," Evan explained. "And, we'll still have the element of surprise. Wherever they're taking him is more than likely under tight security . . . they'll never expect us to be able to breach it. With our superior technology, breaking Tobias out of that place will be easy."

"We'll have to do it that way, now," Trevor said. "The van is driving off."

Evan nodded. "Let it. We'll get him back. Besides, if Braden's correct about this facility, I want to check it out."

"Aha! Now we have the real reason you wanted to wait," Autumn said. "You just want to investigate that facility."

Evan shrugged. "Don't you? Aren't you the least bit curious about what goes on at that place, if such a place exists? If they're as obsessed with extraterrestrial life as Braden says, then they may indeed conduct studies there, and they may not rule out killing the specimen for the purpose of dissection."

"I don't understand this," Braden interrupted. "Your friend is probably being hauled off to some research facility, and we're standing around talking? Shouldn't you be planning something?"

"Oh, we'll get him back, don't you worry," Evan said. "And while we're at it, we'll get a closer look of this research facility of yours." Evan retrieved the transport capsule. When it appeared, he led the way, and the others followed.

"By the way, I never have inane conversations," he told his wife.

CHAPTER NINETEEN

Evan and the others were gathered at the large viewing screen in the control room. They had watched the transport of Tobias as they stood in a huddle. He had been driven to a remote location, transferred to a small jet, and then flown to the relatively unknown research center in Arizona Braden had mentioned.

"I always believed that place was real," Braden stated in awe. "The government won't confirm or deny its existence, but there it is."

"Now we can go and rescue him," Trevor said.

"People who breach the security fence are shot on sight," Braden said. "That's how it is with all such places. Everything is done in secrecy. Very little information ever reaches the public. They don't want us to know."

"We've been shot at before." Evan said with a shrug. "Besides, we won't have to climb over a fence . . . the transport pod can take us directly inside the facility."

"What's the plan?" Trevor asked.

"Standard procedure for rescue operations," Evan replied. "We'll work in pairs. Autumn and I, you and Stella."

"Tobias usually takes out surveillance systems," Trevor said. "I imagine that will now be my task, as I'm the only other security expert."

"You've got it," Evan responded with a nod. "I'll get the weapons." He went off to retrieve their weapons.

"What am I to do?" Braden asked.

"You will remain behind, either here or at your residence," Trevor said over his shoulder as he began programming the coordinates into the transport vehicle.

"But, I want to go," Braden pleaded. "Stella said I've been chosen as one of your human contacts. I even have one of those locator chips in me forearm. She offered me a chance to join your crew when you leave Earth."

"It is not open to debate," Trevor stated tersely.

"This will be a dangerous mission," Autumn said. "We've done this before; you haven't. We can't afford to bring someone new on such a dangerous operation."

"But . . ." Braden's youthful enthusiasm wouldn't allow him to let it go.

"Discussion over," Autumn stated shortly. "And, quite frankly, Evan and I haven't yet approved your joining the ship. In case she hasn't told you, Evan's the captain, and I'm second in command. We will make the final decision."

Stella and Autumn exchanged glances. Stella didn't challenge Autumn's position. Trevor didn't want to get involved.

"Here are the guns," Evan said when he returned. He looked at everyone, and he immediately knew something was up. "Did I miss something?"

"No big deal," Autumn answered with a shrug.

"I know something happened." Evan eyed them each in turn. "Spill it."

"Braden wanted to come," Autumn said. "I told him he couldn't."

"I would keep a close watch on him at all times," Stella interjected. "I would take full responsibility for his actions."

"Absolutely not." Evan shook his head. "Not on something like this."

"I offered him an opportunity to join us. You never refused my requests before, Evan."

"I didn't say he couldn't join, Stella. I said he can't go on this assignment." An uncomfortable silence followed as Stella dropped her gaze, and Braden fidgeted. Trevor looked on curiously.

"I won't need a gun," Autumn said, more to break the silence than anything else.

"I didn't bring you one, dear." Evan grinned at his wife. "Your mind is more powerful than any gun." Autumn made a face as if to say, "don't you know it."

"I don't like guns," Stella said.

"These are stun guns," Evan said. "I have no intention of allowing anyone to be killed down there." He extended one of the stun guns, adding, "Take it . . . that's an order."

Stella took it without further comment.

"Okay, then, let's go rescue Tobias," Evan said.

CHAPTER TWENTY

The transport capsule materialized inside the facility. The door slid open, and out stepped Evan and Autumn. They were in a remote area of the complex, allowing them to enter unseen. The giant silver bell stood silently in the alcove where it had appeared.

"Stay here," Evan stated quietly before slowly making his way out into the open. Satisfied that the coast was clear, he turned his attention back to his wife, gesturing for her to join him.

"We'll lay low until you knock out the power," Evan told Trevor, who was standing in the open doorway of the transport vehicle.

Trevor nodded, and ducked back inside. The door closed, and the big silver bell disappeared with no more than a whisper of sound.

"This place is creepy, Evan," Autumn said as they slowly made their way through the tunnel that served as a corridor. They were deep underground, and the air was stale, cool, and damp. Although she was wearing a heavy sweater, she hugged herself as if cold. The chill she experienced may have had little to do with the elements.

"We'll need your senses on high alert," Evan told her as they walked. His attention was half on where they were going, and half on his mobile device. It was sleek of design, black with red trim. It was like a cellular phone, only far more sophisticated. At the moment, he was studying a schematic of the facility that he'd managed to acquire, thanks to the Solar Flare's ability to hack into any of Earth's computer, satellite, and security systems. The space ship was able to obtain whatever bit of information they needed regarding the top secret research facility. Encrypted files took a little longer to manage, but the human created systems were no match for the Solar Flare.

"I can hear Tobias calling to me. Evan, Braden was right; they're going to kill him. He's a curiosity to these people . . . a bit of proof of the existence of extraterrestrial life elsewhere in the universe."

Evan glanced at his wife. "Don't worry, darling; we'll get him out of here. These people are no match for us."

"I sense something else, Evan," Autumn said. "Something ominous."

Evan looked from his screen with a frown. "What do you mean?"

"There's something here," Autumn explained. "A presence . . . and, it's in pain."

"A presence?" Evan's frown deepened. "And, it's in pain?"

Autumn nodded. She was becoming emotional, looking as if she were sad. "It's afraid, and it's imprisoned here." She turned her worried green eyes to her husband. "Evan, it's telepathic . . . it sensed my presence, and reached out to me with its mind."

"I find that very disturbing," Evan said. "Evidently, Braden was right about this place in more ways than one. No wonder they keep it shrouded in mystery, and few humans even know of its existence."

There was the sound of conversation somewhere up ahead. Two men were walking towards them. Evan and Autumn froze, furtively looking for a place to hide, but there was none. Evan's right hand instantly went for the stun gun at his hip. He drew it, ready to fire when necessary.

The two men rounded the corner. They had been laughing over some shared joke. The laughter and smiles quickly faded when they saw the pair of intruders in their midst.

"What the . . ." One of the men began as they both drew their weapons. Evan zapped both of them before either of them could so much as take aim. They collapsed to the floor in a heap, conscious but unable to move. They looked up at Evan and Autumn in utter shock as the pair stood over them.

"We should put them to sleep," Autumn suggested. "Their nervous systems will recover relatively quickly."

"You may be right; we don't know enough about human physiology yet to trust a stun alone." He changed the setting on his weapon, and zapped both men again. This time, they were rendered unconscious.

"That should keep them out for awhile," Evan said as he holstered his weapon.

"We can't just keep them here," Autumn said. "Suppose others come along and find them? They'll put the entire facility on alert, and they'll know they have intruders here. We'll lose the element of surprise."

Evan nodded in agreement. "We've got to hide them somewhere."

"We may have to disintegrate them," Autumn stated softly.

"No killing unless we have no other choice," Evan said.

"Okay, but what do you have in mind?" Autumn asked. "And, quickly, because we don't have a lot of time."

Evan studied his mobile device, quickly scanning the map of the area. His face brightened when he found a possible solution.

"Here," he said, holding the unit so she could see. "There's a storage room around the corner, on the left." He smiled as he pocketed his device. "Come on, help me with these men. We'll have to drag them along. I'll take the big guy; you take the smaller one."

"Are you kidding me?" Autumn asked, staring incredulously at Evan, who had grabbed the larger man beneath the shoulders.

"What?" Evan asked.

"This guy's nearly as big as that one," Autumn complained. "And, he must be twice my weight."

"More like three times," Evan quipped with a silly grin. "Let's get moving . . . like you said, we haven't time to waste."

Autumn grabbed the smaller guy beneath the shoulders as Evan had done. Then, she started dragging him, walking backwards as she followed her husband. She grunted and grumbled as she struggled with his dead weight. She wasn't able to keep up with her husband, lagging behind more and more as they went.

"Disintegration would have been much easier," she muttered to herself as she huffed and puffed along the way. "Who cares about these humans, anyway?" She asked out loud so that Evan could hear.

"They're planning to kill one of ours, aren't they?"

"Only barbarians kill for no reason," Evan said. "We're not going to stoop to their level."

The storage room was within sight. First, Evan laid his man down on the cold, hard floor. Then, using his weapon, he destroyed the doorknob's locking mechanism. After he holstered his weapon once again, he turned the knob, and pushed open the door. Finally, he grabbed his man, and dragged him inside the room.

Autumn was still halfway down the hall. She had to stop now and then in order to rest. Evan came to her aid as soon as he was finished.

"A little help here would be nice," Autumn stated sarcastically. "I'm five feet tall and I weight a hundred pounds, Evan. It's like an ant trying to move an elephant."

"Ant s are actually quite strong," Evan said as he crouched beside her. "Here, allow me." He smiled, and gave his wife a quick kiss. "You did good, love."

Evan dragged the second man the rest of the way and into the storage room. After closing the door, he used his weapon to fuse the knob so that it could no longer be opened.

"That should keep them out of the way for awhile," he said with a satisfied smile.

"Evan, contact Trevor and find out how much longer before the power's knocked out."

Evan's expression grew concerned when he saw the seriousness on Autumn's face. "Why? What's happened?"

"They're getting ready to study Tobias. He's calling out to me again, pleading for us to help him."

"Let him know we're here, and we're going to get him out."

While Autumn established a telepathic link with Tobias, Evan contacted Trevor. Time was growing short; they had to act, and they had to do it quickly. Otherwise, all they'd be taking back to the ship with them would be Tobias's corpse.

CHAPTER TWENTY-ONE

Trevor stood with his back against the wall in the hall outside the electrical room. The tall, ruggedly built black man was dressed entirely in black: T-shirt, denim pants, and boots. His long black hair curled about his shoulders, and his face was one of determination and deep concentration. He was prepared for anything.

He peered around the corner, and eyed the entrance to the electrical room. The weapon in his holster was set to stun anyone who happened to see him. Evan's orders were firm: no killing unless there was no alternative. That was fine with Trevor; he preferred physical confrontations over weapons, anyway . . . it was more fun that way.

"I have the electrical room in sight," he said into the silver bracelet on his left wrist. "I should have the power off shortly."

"Hurry it up," Stella said. "I'm not al that keen on being alone out here to fend off unwanted guests."

Trevor looked back at her. "You'll do fine. You're trained for battle, and their weaponry if inferior to ours. This shouldn't take long." His gaze lingered on the attractive young woman. She too was dressed all in black: a long sleeved blouse, spandex pants, and running shoes. She stood just behind him, her gaze furtively searching the area. She wasn't paying attention to his lingering stare. Once, they may have had something together. But, what they had begun had burned quickly, like a wildfire out of control until there was nothing left to burn. All that remained was a deep, platonic love; the kind shared between close friends.

Trevor shoved the memories away, and went about his task. As he breached the locks and entered the electrical room, his thoughts turned to Braden. He knew the human was attracted to Stella, and that she was attracted to him. *What does she see in him?* He wondered. He could understand why Braden was drawn to her . . . she was beautiful and intelligent, and there was great power in her touch.

But, why did she like him? What is it about that feeble, inferior human? There was no time to think about such things; he had work to do.

Stella stood watch just outside the double set of doors, her stun gun held limply at her hip in her right hand. She kept looking left to right, and then forward again, hoping she wouldn't have to fight, or worse. She was a healer, a medical doctor . . . the mere thought of causing bodily harm to someone was deplorable to her.

As she stood dutifully at her post, her thoughts drifted to Braden, who was left behind on the Solar Flare. He was watching everything on the large viewing screen in the control room. He wanted to become a member of the crew, and she wanted him to be a part of the team as well. That wasn't all she wanted; she wanted to get him alone in her lab one of these nights, and have at it. She knew he wanted to as well. However, he was rather shy, and intimacy would take some time. She'd had Autumn probe his mind for her. She'd learned of Braden's private erotic thoughts regarding Stella . . . he was just too timid to broach the subject with her.

Enough about Braden! Stella told herself. *There will be plenty of time for that after we get Tobias out of here . . . right now, we have a job to do.*

A pair of maintenance men rounded the corner. Stella's keen hearing had warned her of their impending approach long before their arrival. She tensed, and aimed her weapon.

"Trevor, we've got company," she barked over her shoulder.

She didn't hear Trevor's response. She was too busy firing at the approaching men. It had been all too easy. They were unarmed, and her presence startled them enough to freeze them momentarily. By the time either of them finally managed to react, they were both lying on the floor unconscious.

CHAPTER TWENTY-TWO

E van and Autumn approached the end of the long, winding corridor, which connected with another one that ran from left to right. Seeing a large window on the hall to their right, they went to investigate. They peered in the window, and were utterly astounded by what they saw. Inside the large room were numerous artifacts of extraterrestrial design. It was a storage room for the many finds of human kind regarding alien life. All of it gave humanity ample proof of the existence of intelligent life elsewhere in the universe.

"Will you look at that," Evan stated in awe. "Braden was indeed correct about this place." He frowned, and looked at his wife. "But why don't they want the rest of humanity to know about this?"

Autumn shrugged. "Who knows? I haven't had time to study the human mind. That is, with the exception of Braden and Ryan."

"All I know is," Evan began, "is that whenever we discover something new and exciting, our whole world knows about it."

"Yeah, well, not everyone is as forthcoming as we are," Autumn said. "I'm beginning to think these humans are a bunch of weirdos."

"Want to look inside?" Evan asked with the enthusiasm of a child, eager to take a closer look.

"Evan, we don't have the time. Tobias is about to be dissected, remember?"

"Maybe Stella can put him back together again."

"Evan . . ."

"What? Are you going to tell me you aren't the least bit curious about this?"

"Of course I am. But I'd rather see Tobias remain alive."

"Stella's brought people back to life before," Evan stated with a shrug.

"Not after they've been torn apart into pieces."

Evan peered back through the window. "There's all kinds of gadgets in there. And, I think I see the wreckage of that Space ship Braden mentioned. And, look, there's a stuffed head in a huge showcase . . . it's got big bulbous eyes and a forehead shaped like an egg." He looked back at his wife with the enthusiasm of a child on Christmas morning. "This is astounding, Autumn. These people don't realize what they're into."

There was no time to discuss it further. At that moment, the lights went out.

CHAPTER TWENTY-THREE

"He's in there," Autumn whispered to Evan. The two were huddled together not far from the double set of doors to the examining room. Two men uniform stood on guard duty, one on either side of the doors. They were in blue clothing with darker blue trim, and they wore identical black boots. They stood with their hands behind their backs, silently staring straight ahead. Neither of them noticed Evan and Autumn because of the darkness; the emergency lights cast long shadows on the walls, but Evan and Autumn were too far away to be distinguishable.

"We'll make our move now," Evan said quietly. "Use your telepathy. Show them we have the upper hand."

"Got it."

Evan grabbed her shoulder. "Be firm, but don't reduce their brains to vegetable matter," he added.

"I understand, Evan."

Evan and Autumn stood side by side, and approached the men. The expressions on the faces of the guards were of men taken by surprise. Evan quickly drew his weapon as the men did the same.

"Stop right there!" One of the men in uniform barked in a tone that matched the scowl on his face.

Evan eyed the guns in their hands, then at their faces. "You think you can stop us with those?" He asked. He and Autumn exchanged glances, and they both laughed.

"Freeze!" The guard in charge ordered. "Drop your weapon, mister! And put your hands in the air." The pudgy, middle-aged man glanced it Autumn, adding, "You, too, miss. Hands in the air."

Evan and Autumn looked at each other.

Now? Autumn asked Evan telepathically, and Evan nodded.

"I don't think you're in any position to make demands," Autumn said as she stepped forward. "And, don't think for a moment you can stop me with that useless gun of yours."

"If you don't stop this instant, you're going to find out whether this gun is useless or not," the man retorted. Both men aimed directly at her. Autumn continued her approach, unfazed.

"This is what I think of you and your gun." Autumn smiled wickedly, and took control of his mind. In the next instant, he was bringing his gun up, aiming the barrel in the direction of his head.

His partner's eyes went wide. This second man was taller, leaner, and about ten years younger than the pudgy, middle-aged man in charge.

"Bill, what are you doing?" The junior uniform asked, shock evident in his tone.

"Yes, Billy, what are you doing?" Autumn echoed harshly, knowing full well what was happening. She grinned wickedly as the pudgy, sweating man brought the barrel of the gun closer and closer to his head, pointing it directly at his right temple.

"I . . . can't . . . she's inside my head," the pudgy, frightened man stated through gritted teeth. "I can't control myself! She's in my goddamned head!"

"What the hell are you talking about?" The junior uniform asked, his face contorted in worry. His weapon trembled in his grip, still aimed at Autumn, as he stared in horror at his partner. Knock it off, Bill! This isn't funny!"

"Yeah, this isn't funny," Autumn said, thoroughly enjoying herself. Her wicked smile grew cruel before turning into a cold, heartless laugh.

"Lower your weapon," Evan ordered at the junior guard, "or your partner will blow his own head off, with his own gun."

"D-do as he says, Mark," Bill gasped, his face red, and his expression a pained grimace. "I can't stop her . . . she's going to make me blow my brains out."

"Your partner is telling the truth," Autumn said. "I'm not playing games. Lower your weapon, or he's dead." Of course, she really didn't want to, but she would if it became necessary. She hoped the younger man was scared enough to not call her bluff.

The junior guard lowered his weapon.

"Smart move," Evan said. "Now, put it on the floor, and kick it toward me. One stupid move on your part, and your partner is dead. Do it . . . now."

Mark slowly lowered himself into a crouch, and gently set his weapon on the floor. Then, after he got back to his feet, he kicked it toward Evan. Evan picked it up, and eyed the primitive human weapon curiously. Then, he tucked it in a pocket of his black, imitation leather jacket.

"How many are in there?" Autumn asked. "In that rom? And don't lie, or I'll do something even worse to you than I did to your partner." Autumn glanced at the pudgy man, who was still standing at his post, trembling and trying to gather himself. His gun was now pointed at the floor instead of his head.

"You, too," Evan ordered. "Set your gun on the floor, and kick it to me." The shaken man complied, glad to be rid of the piece.

Evan picked up the gun, and put it in his other coat pocket. "Gentlemen, I regret having to do this, but . . ."

"No!" The pudgy uniform exclaimed.

"Don't kill us," his partner said. "We did as you asked."

"If we wanted to kill you, you'd be dead already," Evan said before quickly dropping them with his stun gun. Both men collapsed to the floor in a heap on either side of the door.

"Uh, I asked him a question, Evan."

Evan shrugged. "It doesn't matter if there are a dozen people in there. They're no match for us."

They burst into the room, and several sets of eyes widened upon seeing them enter. There were six people, four men and two women, gathered around an large oval table. Three were on one side, the other three were on the other. Lying in the center of the table, on his back, was Tobias. He was unconscious. There were two more people, a man and a woman, standing inside the double set of doors, one on either side of it, like the two out in the hall.

The person in charge, an old man with white hair and wire framed eyeglasses, looked up from studying Tobias as if to scold the guards for entering, but he too stared incredulously at the intruders.

"Who are you?" The old man asked when he'd recovered himself. "And, how did you get past the guards?"

"I'm afraid your guards are sleeping at their posts," Evan commented with an air confidence. "Would you like to step out of the room and see for yourself?"

"Unfortunately for you," the old man countered, "we have two more in here." Looking to the uniformed man and woman, he barked, "Apprehend them, and put them in cuffs. Then, call the authorities, and have them arrested."

"I'm afraid we can't allow that to happen," Evan said. As the two guards started toward them, Evan zapped the man with his stun gun. Autumn looked a the woman, and took control of her mind. The woman's eyes went wide, and she dropped her gun. For no apparent reason, the woman was terrified. Her eyes went wide, and she screamed.

When things started flying around the room, all of the others froze. It was the work of Autumn, who was using her telekinetic power to move inanimate objects sailing across the room, mostly medical apparatus such as scalpels and stethoscopes. Chairs tipped over, and cabinet doors began opening and closing in rapid succession, slamming and flinging open again as if unseen hands were at work in the room. People screamed and shouted, scattering about as they sought cover. Autumn and Evan laughed, thoroughly enjoying the spectacle.

"Scurrying away like a bunch of scared rats," Autumn said with an amused grin.

"Don't anybody move!" Evan demanded firmly, "or it won't be the only furniture my wife throws around." He and Autumn hurried toward the table to where Tobias lay. Evan examined him while Autumn looked on, prepared to act should any of the humans become brave enough to come out of hiding. Nobody did.

"I don't think they got very far with him," Evan said, satisfied that Tobias hadn't been harmed. "But, we should have Stella look him over just to be sure." He spoke into his communication wrist bracelet. "Trevor, Stella, what is your location?"

"We're headed in your direction now," Trevor replied. "They had a backup generator that took over when I took out the main power,' he continued. "I had to disable that as well."

"Good work. They didn't know what hit them. Apparently, there's yet another backup system somewhere, because the room that we're in has power."

"Did you find Tobias? Is he all right?" Stella asked.

"He's seems okay," Evan answered. "They've got him asleep. I think we got to him in time. You should take a look at him to make sure."

"More people are coming," Autumn said. "And, in force."

"We should leave here as quickly as possible. Autumn says reinforcements are coming, and in large numbers," Evan told Stella and Trevor.

"We heard her," Trevor said. "We have your location in sight now . . . we'll be right there."

"I'll get the transport here," Evan said, already retrieving it via his mobile device.

"Evan, what about that entity I told you about?" Autumn asked. "The one who called out to me; the one that's suffering somewhere in this place? We can't just leave until we find out what it's all about."

"Autumn, this is a huge complex. We have to get out before the reinforcements arrive in order to avoid bloodshed. You'll have to locate this thing . . . whatever it is, quickly."

"I believe I can locate it, and it won't take long."

Evan nodded. "All right, we'll try. But if I think it's taking too long, we're leaving."

"Fair enough," Autumn said.

Trevor and Stella entered the room just as the transport capsule appeared, just inside the room and to the left of the doors. They glanced at the big silver bell, then hurried over to Evan and Autumn. Trevor surveyed the room while Stella ran her medical scanner over Tobias.

"He's unharmed," Stella said, sounding relieved. "I was worried we wouldn't get to him before they . . ." She left her statement go unfinished.

"Let's get him back to the ship, where you can give him a thorough examination just to be sure," Evan said.

As he picked up the little winged man and started to carry him away, one of the guards aimed his gun in their direction. Sensing it, Autumn used telekinesis to take the weapon from his grasp and into her hand. Then, with the gleaming firearm in her palm, she sent it back in his direction, so fast it was no more than a blur as it flew through the air. The gun then struck the guard hard in the head. He cried out, then fell eerily silent. He'd been knocked unconscious by his own gun.

"The next one stupid enough to move will get even worse than that," Autumn announced for the benefit of the other humans. "Consider yourselves warned."

"You humans aren't very bright," Evan said to the crouching, cowering people scattered about the room, beneath tables, in closets, and behind file cabinets. "Stay put, and nobody gets hurt," he added.

Evan carried Tobias into the transport capsule. He was quickly followed by Autumn and Stella. Trevor took up the rear, his weapon drawn and ready to fire should any of the humans try anything. None of them did. The door of the pod slid shut, and the big silver bell disappeared. The humans watched in utter astonishment, wondering who in the world possessed such incredible technology. They couldn't believe it, and neither could the reinforcements when they arrived. The story they'd ben told by the frightened people in the room was just too crazy to believe.

CHAPTER TWENTY-FOUR

The telepathic entity Autumn had sensed was actually a person. Or, rather, it was the head of a person. It was located in another room in the sprawling underground complex. Autumn had managed to find the head with her telepathy. The creature spoke to Autumn telepathically, and Autumn knew where to go. It was similar to following someone's voice, only the words weren't spoken aloud. The had shared a telepathic link.

The head was of a humanoid female. It was alive, and it was staring back a them through a transparent barrier set into a wall. They all stared at the head in wonder. It, or rather, she, had numerous cables and metallic instruments attached to her head, and at the base of her neck. The tubes and cables ran into the wall. They were implanted in her in order to allow the human scientists to interact with her. Her brain was literally wired into the mainframe of a complex computer system.

The humanoid female was sickly pale, and her features bore a striking resemblance to Stella. The only exceptions were that the woman had black hair instead of dark brown, and her eyes were midnight blue instead of brown. Her long hair gathered at the base of her neck, shrouding whatever lie beneath it.

"Will you look at that!" Autumn exclaimed in awe.

"Look what they've done to her," Stella said, becoming emotional by what she saw. "And, she looks like me!"

"These humans are a barbaric race." Trevor shook his head in disgust.

"There's no way this primitive society is capable of an operation of this complexity," Evan said. He frowned. "And, you're not kidding! She does look like you . . . she could be your twin."

"She's suffering," Autumn said sadly. "She's from a distant world . . . she was part of an exploration vessel that arrived here fifteen Earth years ago. She and her shipmates were captured . . . she's the only survivor.' Autumn turned tearful eyes to the others. "They were tortured and killed. She was kept alive so they could extract knowledge from her. They keep her alive artificially." Looking at her husband, she added, "Evan, this is a chamber of horrors. What are we going to do about it?"

"What can we do?" He asked. "There isn't time. More humans are coming, and they're going to search ever inch of this place until they find us."

"We have to get out of here if we intend to maintain our anonymity, and avoid killing anyone when we're forced to defend ourselves," Trevor said.

"We've managed to not kill anyone so far," Autumn reasoned. "The humans scare easily. Evan, yo saw their reaction when I was throwing things across the room with my mind. We'll do it again if we have to."

"We could destroy this entire complex in a matter of minutes," Evan said. "But not without killing humans. Barbarians or not, I don't want deaths unless it's absolutely necessary."

"Can we rescue her?" Stella asked. "Move her? Take her back with us?"

"We can try," Evan replied. He was already studying the holding compartment in search of a way to do it. Trevor joined him, doing the same.

"It's self contained," Evan said. They constructed whatever this is around her . . . head."

"It's built into the wall," Trevor added with a shake of the head. "Moving this would be nearly impossible."

"And, it would take lots of time,' Evan said.

"Which we don't have," Trevor said.

"Are you telling me there's nothing we can do?" Autumn asked. "Us? With all of our technology, and having the most powerful spaceship in the galaxy at our disposal?"

"Autumn, we can reduce this place to rubble, but we can't move the . . . lady here without major work. That work will take time." Evan was very sympathetic, and he understood his wife's outrage completely. However, for the moment, at least, there was not much they could do.

"We could come back for her later," Trevor suggested, "after we've put some sort of a plan together. Evan's right; we've got to get out of here, and we need special apparatus in order to move her."

Autumn didn't want to admit it, but they were right.

"Fine," she said shortly. "But we come back at the earliest opportunity. Sooner or later, they'll kill her, too."

"Where's the rest of her body?" Stella wondered aloud.

Autumn was about to ask, but her senses picked up approaching humans.

"They're coming,' she said.

"Let's go," Evan said. "We'll come back." Looking at the pale female with long black hair and sorrowful blue eyes behind the transparent barrier, he added, "I promise."

They stepped into the waiting transport, and then they disappeared. The humanoid female head behind the transparent barrier watched them leave, tears streaming down her cheeks. She hoped they would keep their promise. She wanted out of this place before she suffered the same fate as her shipmates.

Several armed men barged into the room shortly after the big silver bell disappeared. They looked around, looking disappointed at not finding the intruders. The humanoid female head watched them leave. As the doors closed, she prayed the others would come back. If they didn't come back for her, she hoped that she did. It would be better to die than to continue to exist in this hellish place.

CHAPTER TWENTY-FIVE

They returned to the Solar Flare shortly thereafter. They were surprised to see that Braden wasn't in the control room when they stepped out of the transport and onto the deck.

"Braden's not here," Stella said, looking around the large oval room for any sign of him.

"He's not officially part of the crew yet, and already he's disobeying orders," Trevor commented gruffly.

Evan walked to the command center. Switching on the communication link, he said, "Braden, this is Evan. Where are you?"

There was no response. Evan repeated himself, but there was still no answer.

"He's up top, in the botanical garden," Autumn said.

"You can sense him up there?" Evan asked.

"No, the Solar Flare told me."

He was indeed in the botanical garden. They found him near the fountain, lying on one of the stone benches, encased in lush green, prickly vines. He was whimpering, and begging the vines to let him go.

"Oh, isn't that cute?" Stella asked as they approached. "They made a blanket of themselves to keep him warm."

"Let me out of here! These things have a mind of their own! The more I try to get up, the tighter they become!"

"Be nice, and let Braden up," Stella gently scolded. "What have I told you about scaring the guests?"

"You're talking to them as if they understand," Braden said, trembling with fear.

"They do understand." Stella slapped at the vines, which were already starting to retreat. "What were you doing up here, anyway?"

"You called me up here. Or, I thought you did. I mean, I would have sworn you did. It was your voice I heard over the intercom."

"The Solar Flare did it," Autumn said. "Our ship was playing a game with you." She smiled. Or rather, she sneered.

"Playing a game? I thought those things were going to strangle me to death! And, those creepy red eyes kept staring at me through those bushes." He pointed at the large bush nearby, where Red Eye was hiding.

"Calm down, Braden," Stella said. "You're overreacting. There's nothing on this space ship that would wish to harm you."

"Still want to be a part of our family?" Evan asked.

"Family?" Braden looked confused. "You mean, you're all related?"

"Not by blood. But it isn't blood alone that makes a family," Evan responded. "We know people who are blood related that aren't much of a family at all. We all care about each other here . . . we fight side by side, and are willing to sacrifice our lives for the sake of the others. We're together, and we can't imagine our lives with one of us not here. So, as far as we're concerned, we're family."

Braden nodded. "I get it. And, I'm sorry I freaked. It's going to take time to get used to this . . . alien way of life."

"Well, you're welcome to join us, if you wish," Evan said. "My wife and I discussed it, and we're okay with it."

"Yeah, because we know it would make Stella happy," Autumn added. "For some crazy reason we don't understand, she likes you, and wants to keep you around."

"Yeah," Braden said, exchanging smiles with Stella. "I'd like that."

"Perhaps you should go home and ask mommy and daddy first," Trevor said with a smirk. "Our way of life can be rather frightening and dangerous at times. It's not for the faint of heart."

"Yeah, I'm sure," Braden said. Actually, he wasn't so sure.

CHAPTER TWENTY-SIX

Ryan parked his car in the driveway, and climbed out of the vehicle with briefcase in hand. He closed the door, secured the lock, and started toward the house. It had been a long, exciting day, not so much at the office, but rather, in the news. Tobias was still the dominant news item; however, the others had begun to be noticed as well. Video footage of their giant silver bell appearing and disappearing was beginning to appear on the internet, and there was some unsubstantiated news that they were involved in an incident at a top secret research facility known as Area Six, in the open plains of Arizona.

Ryan approached the door, hoping he could talk about it with his wife. That is, if she would discuss it with him. She still wasn't convinced regarding his night spent on board an alien space ship, and she still believed he didn't need eye glasses anymore because he'd had laser surgery done on his eyes. He really wished that little redheaded snot of an alien would do like she said she would, and fix his marital problems.

Ryan was about to open the door when it unexpectedly opened for him. On the other side stood his wife, smiling and seemingly pleased to see him. The sight was so startling to him that he momentarily froze.

"Well, er, hello, dear," he stammered, not knowing what to think.

"Hello, love," Tiffany replied. Stepping back, she gestured for him to enter. "What are you waiting for? Come on in."

"Hello, love?" Ryan was flabbergasted. He eyed her up and down, adding, "Why are you all dolled up?"

"Can't a woman dress nice for her husband?" She was wearing a blue dress cut to the knees, with matching pumps. The shoes had open toes and heels, with a strap wrapping around the ankle. Her collar length blond hair was freshly dyed and newly styled. She wore just a hint of make up, and she looked positively stunning. Ryan was beside himself, not knowing what to make of it.

"I missed you," she said, leaning in for a kiss. It was the first kiss they'd shared for nearly a week. "Come into the kitchen; I have a surprise for you."

Ryan watched her walk away, hesitating for a moment. Her form fitting dress showed off her curves as she walked, and Ryan couldn't help but stare. Finally, he managed to follow.

The kitchen smelled of simmering sauce and boiling pasta. There were burning scented candles on the table, and their finest dinnerware was set. The thing he noticed next was that the table was only set for two.

"Uh, there are only two places set," he said as he watched her at the stove, stirring the simmering pasta sauce. "And, what's up with the candles?"

"The kids are staying at mu sister's tonight, and the candles are for our dinner." She looked at her husband, appearing the slightest bit annoyed. But then, her expression softened as he said, "Take off your suit jacket, and sit down at the table. Dinner will be ready shortly."

"Tiffany, what's going on?"

Tiffany looked at him as if she couldn't understand why he didn't get it. "We're going to have a nice, candle lit dinner, and then we're going to have an even better, romantic evening . . . just the two of us, no kids, no interruptions."

"Uh . . . Tiffany? Did a petite redheaded woman stop by today, by any chance?"

"Why, yes! She's such an adorable little thing." Tiffany smiled pleasantly. "She and I had a little talk."

"A little . . . talk?" *She used her telepathy, no doubt,* Ryan thought.

"Yes, and she confirmed everything you told me." Tiffany stopped stirring, and covered the pan. Her blue eyes locked onto his, and his stomach tightened.

She went to her husband, and took him into her embrace. "Oh, Ryan, I'm sorry I doubted you. I'll never doubt you again." She kissed him for a second time, and this time it was long and more passionate. She pressed her body into his, just like she sued to. Ryan couldn't believe it was happening.

What the hell has that little redheaded alien done? Ryan wondered.

He was about to find out.

CHAPTER TWENTY-SEVEN

Evan and Autumn were sitting on a park bench in the same small, New England city they'd been visiting all along. The air was pleasantly warm, and the sun was shining. Puffy white clouds slowly drifted by in the otherwise clear blue sky overhead. They were sitting close together, each with an arm around the other. It felt good to have some quiet alone time after all of the turmoil since they'd awakened from suspended animation nearly a week ago.

"I think I might actually like this place," Autumn said with her head resting against Evan's shoulder.

"Yes, it reminds me of home," Evan replied. "Did you fix Ryan's situation?" He asked.

"Of course, Evan. I always keep my promises. Ryan and his wife are enjoying wedded bliss once again." She frowned, adding, I do hope Stella did a thorough job restoring Ryan's health . . . I would hate for something to happen to him during an act of passion."

Evan looked at his wife. "You have an evil mind," he said with a smile.

"A practical mind," Autumn corrected. "By the way, what about that poor tortured woman at that chamber of horrors we encountered? Are we going after to her?"

"A promise is a promise," Evan said. "We'll rescue her as soon as we can."

They sat in silence for awhile, enjoying the alone time as well as the sights and sounds of nature around them. They watched people as they went by either on foot or in motor vehicles. Autumn sighed contentedly.

"Happy?" Evan asked.

"Yes. And, why not? All is right in our world again; we're alive and well, we have a place to lay low for awhile, and our ship is making steady repairs."

"I can't argue with that." Evan bent to kiss his wife, and their lips met. Their pleasant quiet time came to a halt, however, when a familiar black luxury car pulled up to the curb. It was Ryan.

"Hey, guys," he stated joyfully as he climbed out of his car, looking at them with a huge grin on his face. "Fancy meeting you here."

"Yeah, we'll have to find some other place to be alone, I guess," Autumn said with mild sarcasm.

"I just wanted to thank you for your help," Ryan told Autumn. "My wife and I are good again."

"You're welcome."

"I mean, last we . . . . ah, you know, we . . ."

"I know. I planned it."

"Tiffany and I had one heck of a night last night."

"Happy to hear it."

"I mean, we did it like no tomorrow. I mean, it was hot. We . . ."

"Please, spare me the sordid details," Autumn said with a sour face, holding up a hand for him to stop. "You had a good time, I get it."

Evan observed the exchange with an amused expression on his face.

"Is that all, Ryan?" Autumn asked. "You aren't the only one who enjoys romantic time. My husband and I would like to be left in peace."

Ryan's face darkened. "There's something I think you both should know," he said.

"Oh? What's that?" Autumn asked.

"You people had better keep a low profile for a time, if you still intend to remain anonymous around here," he said.

"Is that so?"

"Yes. You're all over the news," Ryan went on. "Your Tobias has created quite a stir. And, your big silver bell is all over the news as well."

"Gee, we'd never have known," Autumn responded sarcastically. "Do you have any other valuable advice for us, Ryan?"

Ryan frowned, annoyed by Autumn's smugness. "No, but I do have something to say."

Autumn gave him the raised eyebrows look.

"You people are . . . are a bunch of . . ."

"Cosmic wonders?"

"Cosmic misfits! That's what you are," Ryan said. "You're a bunch of nutty, cosmic misfits. Especially you, you little redheaded . . ."

"What?" Autumn prompted, daring him to say it.

Ryan laughed. "Nothing. Nothing, my dear. I can't possibly stay mad at you, even though you put me through hell."

"Do you forgive me?" Autumn couldn't care less whether he did or not. As far as she was concerned, they were even. He revived them and helped them, and she returned the favor . . . big time.

"Of course,' Ryan replied. "Have a good day." He smiled and nodded at Evan, then at Autumn. He turned away, and, speaking over his shoulder, he said, "Besides, you can't help it . . . you're just a playful little alien mischief maker, that's all." With that, Ryan left them alone.

Autumn and Evan watched him drive away. Autumn laughed.

"What's so funny?" Evan asked.

"Ryan. We have to invite him up for a party sometime. He'd make good for good fun." She smiled at Evan with a gleam in her eyes. "I wonder how he'd fare in the botanical garden?"

"Don't even think about it," Evan said.

Autumn laughed again. Ryan had pegged them right. The were indeed cosmic misfits.

And, their adventures on our little blue world were just beginning.